"Call me crazy, but I'm actually feeling relieved now."

"Relieved? How are you relieved? Because the prank wasn't aimed at you?"

"No. Because you weren't the one who was the instigator. For a while there I thought maybe you really disliked me, or at least that you didn't want me opening the spa. I want to make sure you're sticking around this time because you see the potential in what I'm doing and not because of some misplaced sense of obligation. That stupid auction means nothing. You know that, right?"

Nick glanced over at Vivian. She was such a striking woman, with her golden hair silhouetted against the moonlight in the dark cab, that his breath snagged in his throat. He wasn't certain he was staying for *all* the right reasons…definitely not for the genuine motives Vivian was suggesting.

No—he was starting to think he was sticking around for the *wrong* reasons. He was feeling all muddled up inside his head. Confused. Part of him felt like bolting. And yet he couldn't even consider walking away.

A *Publishers Weekly* bestselling and award-winning author of over forty novels, with almost two million books in print, **Deb Kastner** enjoys writing contemporary inspirational Western stories set in small communities. Deb lives in beautiful Colorado with her husband, miscreant mutts and curious kitties. She is blessed with three adult daughters and two grandchildren. Her favorite hobby is spoiling her grandchildren, but she also enjoys reading, watching movies, listening to music (The Texas Tenors are her favorite), singing in the church choir and exploring the Rocky Mountains on horseback.

Mistletoe Daddy

Deb Kastner

LOVE INSPIRED

INSPIRATIONAL ROMANCE

LOVE INSPIRED®

INSPIRATIONAL ROMANCE

Recycling programs
for this product may
not exist in your area.

ISBN-13: 978-1-335-42441-9

Mistletoe Daddy

First published in 2016. This edition published in 2021.

Copyright © 2016 by Debra Kastner

This edition published by arrangement with Harlequin Books S.A.

For questions and comments about the quality of this book, please contact us
at CustomerService@Harlequin.com.

Love Inspired
22 Adelaide St. West, 40th Floor
Toronto, Ontario M5H 4E3, Canada
www.Harlequin.com

Printed in U.S.A.

Through Him then, let us continually offer God
a sacrifice of praise, that is, the fruit of lips
that confess His name. Do not neglect to
do good and to share what you have;
God is pleased with sacrifices of that kind.
—*Hebrews* 13:15–16

For Isabella and Anthony,
who show by your innocent faith what it really
means to make loving sacrifices to the Lord.

Chapter One

"Texas men are built like bricks and so good lookin', don't you think? Especially these here McKenna boys," elderly Jo Spencer crowed. The cheerful crowd gathered on the community green for the first annual Bachelors and Baskets auction clapped their agreement.

Jo swept her arm, gesturing from the top of Nick's black cowboy hat down to the toes of his boots. "Just feast your eyes on this handsome guy."

Vivian Grainger was definitely looking, though *feasting* wouldn't have been the word she would have used.

Critically assessing would be more accurate. She was trying to decide if Nick McKenna was the right man for the construction contractor job she had to fill. After all, that's what made this auction different from most of the ones she'd heard of before. The organizers weren't auctioning off *dates* with the men who had volunteered. Even the married men were auctioning themselves off for charity. Instead, the men agreed to perform some task or chore for the women who "bought" them. One of Nick's brothers, Slade, had been the first man auctioned off, and when his wife, Laney, won him, she'd announced that he'd be doing dishes and laundry for a month. In turn, the ladies offered a picnic lunch for their winning bid—hence the Bachelors and Baskets theme.

Vivian could handle her own dishes and laundry, but building construction was out of her skill set. Was Nick up for the job? She knew he was a rancher by trade, but from what she'd heard around town, he had major skills in carpentry and remodeling. Vivian needed to shave costs wherever she could but didn't want to sacrifice on quality, since her shop would be her main career focus for the rest of her working life.

"You think his brothers Slade and Jax have muscles?" Jo asked with a delighted cackle. The auction had been Jo's brainchild in the first place, a way to help raise funds for a new long-term care facility and senior center for Serendipity, so naturally she was emceeing the event. And she was clearly taking great delight in parading all these handsome men across her platform.

Jo prodded Nick's biceps with an appreciative whistle that made a dash of color rise to the poor man's face—or at least as much of his face as Vivian could see under his dark layer of scruffy whiskers. Viv's fingers itched to grab a pair of shears and a straight razor and clean him up a bit, if nothing else so she could see what she was really buying. She smothered a chuckle.

"Nick here is the biggest, brawniest of the three McKennas, and let me tell you, that's really saying something."

Indeed, it was, Viv thought with a smirk. All three McKenna brothers stood head and shoulders over most of the other men in Serendipity, and with Nick's deeply tanned, unshaven face and thick black hair long enough to brush the collar of his blue-checked Western shirt, he looked more like a mountain man than a rancher. What really made him stand out were his blue eyes, a pop of color against a background of darkness.

Not that she noticed.

Vivian flipped open her notepad and yanked out the pencil that was holding her bun together, causing a waterfall of straight bleached-blond hair to cascade down her shoulders. If a person looked close enough they might see the thinnest stripe of bright pink on a strand of hair on the right, Vivian's little gift to herself to make her stand out from her identical twin sister, Alexis. Viv had always been the wilder of the two, and even now Alexis was settled down with a husband while Vivian...

Wasn't. And she wasn't going to acknowledge the twinge in her gut whenever she thought about it, either.

She threw her head to the side to brush her hair off of her face and eyed the list she'd made in anticipation of the auction. She immediately checked off several items, just as she'd known she would. She'd narrowed down the list of potential candidates from the list of eligible bachelors that had been posted at Cup O' Jo's Café a week before the auction. Nick was currently at the top of her inventory list.

Strong?

Yes, Nick McKenna was pure, lean, unadulterated muscle. There was not an inch of flab on his whole body. She scratched through that requirement. Nick didn't even need to flex his powerful biceps for them to ripple underneath the rolled-up sleeves of his shirt. Tall and broad-shouldered, Vivian guessed that he stood around six foot four and weighed a good 220 pounds at least. Those beefy arms of his were practically bigger than her waist—or at least, her prepregnancy midsection. At three months along, her once-tiny tummy was now starting to swell with new life.

She laid a protective hand over her abdomen. She wouldn't be able to hide her secret from the public much longer, which was exactly why she needed help to get her business up and running, and the sooner, the better. In this day and age a single mother didn't stand out as much as she once would have, but even if no one else judged her, it made a difference to her. She had betrayed everything she had once believed in, even when she knew it was wrong. She was ashamed to return to her hometown unmarried and pregnant, but with no way to provide for her baby, she'd had no other choice.

Creating a successful business, proving

she could make a good life for her and her child, would hopefully show the folks she knew and loved that she meant to make her life right with God. From this point forward, there was no way to go but up.

But was Nick the right one to help her?

She'd been told he was good with a hammer. His ability to remodel was the most important qualification she required and it was the reason Nick was at the top of her list. She'd asked around town and had discovered he'd not only overseen the remodeling of his mother's house but had built from the ground up two adjacent cabins on his ranch land for himself and one of his brothers.

He knew construction and carpentry, which was just what she needed.

It was *not* one of her conditions that he be handsome…

Jo seemed to think that was the most important prerequisite in a man—any man. Vivian chuckled under her breath and tapped the eraser against her bottom lip thoughtfully as she evaluated the man standing square-shouldered on the auction block, his expression grim but confident.

No, Nick wasn't handsome. Not in the classic sense of the word, anyway. Still, Vivian had to wonder why Serendipity's single ladies weren't bidding up a storm on him right now. He wasn't Vivian's type, by any means, but if a woman liked the rugged-cowboy look—and she knew that many in Serendipity did—he fit the bill perfectly.

Granted, he could do with a haircut and a shave, which was both amusing and ironic, given the project she had in mind for him to help her build.

A beauty salon and spa. She couldn't help but smile to herself.

She knew that many of the single women in the crowd intended to bid on attractive, unattached bachelors not for help with projects, but for love's sake, or at least the possibility of it. But dating and falling in love was the farthest thing from Vivian's mind.

It didn't matter to her at all that Nick wasn't classically handsome. His attractiveness, or lack of, wasn't even on her list, and with good reason.

She wanted nothing—*nothing*—to do with men, handsome or otherwise. She'd been burned to a crisp in her last relationship. Her ex-boyfriend, Derrick, wouldn't even acknowledge that the baby she now carried was his, rejecting both her and their precious offspring.

It was no wonder she didn't trust men as far as she could throw them. Hopefully Nick wasn't looking for a relationship through participating in the auction, because if her bid won he would be sadly disappointed if he was. Viv's thoughts were purely business oriented. That her money was going to fund a good cause—the town senior center—made her investment all the more worthwhile.

Her intention was to try and save a few dollars by not having to hire a professional contractor. Instead, she would use a skillful amateur who knew what he was doing and could get the job done as quickly and easily as possible.

"Which of you lovely young ladies out there is going to open their purses for this fine fellow?" Jo urged when no one jumped forward to bid on Nick. "Shame on you. What's taking you so long?"

Viv paused and swallowed hard, wondering if she really wanted to do this. She only knew Nick in passing—but that was enough to know he had a reputation for being as surly as the grizzly bear he resembled if you caught him in a bad mood. And based on that scowl on his face, he was in a lousy mood right now. Did she really want to inflict that on herself?

She could turn around and walk away from this auction right now and hire a professional to do the work on her salon—someone from out of town who wouldn't know or judge her—but with all the extra expenses of having a newborn, she needed to save money every way she could. She squeezed her eyes shut and raised her hand.

"Three hundred dollars." She grimaced when her voice came out high and squeaky.

She'd planned to bid low to start, expecting there to be other ladies throwing their hats into the loop. She wasn't sure what a bachelor like Nick would go for, but three hundred seemed a reasonable guess. She had five hundred dollars in her pocket and was prepared to bid higher, but she was still having second thoughts about bidding for Nick at all. Maybe she needed to rethink this and select someone less intimidating. There was something about Nick that unnerved her.

Deciding she wouldn't bid any higher, she waited for another woman to raise the stakes and let her off the hook. Surely Nick was worth more than she'd offered. Someone truly interested in him would be sure to bid more. She held her breath.

And waited.

It was so silent she could have heard a barrette drop. She slowly counted to ten, but no one else spoke up.

Which meant she was stuck with Nick, whether she wanted to be or not.

Vivian briefly considered backing out of her bid, but she didn't want to make a big production out of this. The last thing she wanted was to call extra attention to herself, and she didn't want to embarrass Nick. It wasn't his fault she was feeling wishy-washy.

She'd made her choice and, for better or for worse, she was going to stick with it. She shouldn't second-guess herself. This was a better option than hiring a professional. And while there were other men on the docket she could have bid for instead, Nick had the best credentials for what she needed, so Nick it would be.

"Are you serious?" Nick asked the crowd when no one piped up with a higher amount. He gestured with his fingers, encouraging further bids. "Somebody? Anybody?"

Clearly he expected the women in the crowd to be clamoring for his time and attention. How conceited was that? And what was so wrong with her that he wanted to get bids from anybody else? Viv didn't know whether or not she should be offended, but frankly, the way he was acting hurt her feelings. He was practically begging for anyone else besides her to bid on him.

Was she really that bad?

Then again, it could be that he was just trying to make more money for the senior center. She considered that notion for a moment and then tossed it aside, going back to her conclusion that he had a big ego to go along with that big head of his. He probably thought the ladies ought to be crawling all over themselves with the opportunity to win him in an auction.

Vivian scoffed. If that was what he was waiting for, it looked as if it was going to be a long time in coming. She almost felt sorry for him.

Almost.

"Do I hear three-fifty?" Jo asked. This time she didn't wait long for someone else to chime in, not that it seemed like anyone would. "No? Your loss, ladies, and a big win for Miss Vivian Grainger. Welcome back to town, Viv, by the way."

Vivian smiled and waved her thanks. For the welcome. Not for the win.

Jo raised her gavel.

Nick frowned.

"Going once. Going twice." The gavel swept down and landed solidly on the podium. "Sold to Vivian Grainger for three hundred dollars."

The crowd clapped politely but Vivian noticed they were more subdued than they had been with previous entries, especially when it came to the single ladies in town who Vivian had expected to be her biggest competition. Either she hadn't bid high enough or Nick had ticked off a lot of women. Another thought occurred to her. Could the lack of enthusiasm be because of *him*? Her bid wasn't any less than others had made, but she hadn't overextended, either. She could have easily been outbid, if Nick were the trophy he seemed to think he was.

She'd been in middle school when he'd attended high school. He was five years older than her, so it wasn't as if they ran in the same circles. She remembered him being popular, especially with the girls, but he'd never put much effort into his social relationships. He'd always appeared more interested in working his ranch and spending time with his family than in participating in school and community activities.

Apparently some things hadn't changed.

Viv met the gaze of her twin sister, one of the few who knew of Viv's pregnancy. Alexis twirled her hand in the air as if holding a lasso, reminding Vivian that her part in this crazy town event wasn't going to be finished when she handed over her money. Alexis, seated in front of the platform with a fishing tackle box for a cash register, was collecting the money from the winning bids, so Viv inched her way forward through the thick crowd to reach her sister.

Vivian wasn't thrilled about what was expected of her next. *Jo Spencer and her crazy ideas.* Roping the cowboy was a silly gesture concocted to amuse the crowd. Alexis handed her a rope with which she was supposed to lasso her "win."

Nick did nothing to encourage her, standing stock-still, his hands jammed into the front pockets of his blue jeans and his square, dimpled chin jaunting upward. His expression was frozen into a frown, his dark brow lowered over icy blue eyes that Vivian refused to meet.

If he was trying to intimidate her, it wasn't working, because she wasn't about to let him get under her skin. If, however, he was trying to be as immobile as a fence post to make it *easier* for her to lasso him, he was doing a very good job of it.

The problem was, Vivian didn't know how to lasso a post—or anything else, for that matter. Other than playing with a toy nylon rope with Alexis when they were children, she'd never even thrown a lasso.

The fact that Nick wasn't moving might be considerate on his part—although she had serious doubts about that, since he was practically glowering at her—but for all the good it did her, he might as well have been tearing around the stage, trying to dodge her every effort.

She glanced down at the rope in her fist and then back at Nick. The cheering crowd was getting impatient, throwing friendly taunts and barbs about pretty ladies and stubborn cowboys as they waited for her to act.

Well, there was more than one way to skin a fish. Based on what she'd observed so far, there weren't really any ground rules on the roping-the-cowboy part of the equation. She figured she could do it any way she wanted.

Intent on her actions, Viv loosened the loop on the rope and marched up to Nick with a nervous smile. He seemed even bigger up close, his blue-checked Western shirt rippling in the breeze against the black T-shirt that covered his expansive chest. His poor mother, raising three boys this size. She would hate to have seen the grocery bill when they were all under the same roof. It was a good thing he was a rancher. The man must eat an entire cow every week.

With two hands on the lasso, she reached up to ring it over his head, but even on tiptoe she couldn't quite reach high enough to flip the coil over, and his stupid hat was getting in the way.

Their eyes met and she gasped softly. Eyes the color of dark-wash blue jeans completely captured her awareness. She was so taken by his gaze that for several blinks of an eye she forgot what she was doing, forgot the clamoring crowd watching them, forgot even to breathe.

"Get along, little doggy," someone called from the anxiously waiting audience.

Laughter jolted Vivian back to life and she huffed in exasperation. Was Nick ever going to help her here?

Stubborn man. He just stood there hulking over her, unmoving, his massive chest and broad shoulders like a brick wall in front of her and no less giving.

"Give me a break," she muttered loud enough for his ears only. "Can you not just—" She gestured for him to bow his head. A little effort on his part would be nice.

He lifted a brow and one corner of his mouth, and after a long pause, removed his black cowboy hat and crouched low enough for her to reach over the top of him.

"Moo," he said, and grinned wholeheartedly.

The crowd erupted into laughter.

He waved his hat and acknowledged the townspeople as if he hadn't just spent the last who-knows-how-long thwarting her efforts to rope him.

"Don't push it, buster." She sniffed, indignant, and arranged the lasso around his shoulders, tightening it so she could *finally* lead him off the platform. The delighted assembly whistled and applauded.

Two could play at that game. She turned to the crowd and curtsied, letting the enormous sway of her emotions go with the cool Texas breeze. It wasn't in her nature to take herself too seriously or hold a grudge for more than a moment.

Nick, on the other hand, grunted and practically jerked the rope from her hand so he could pull the lasso off himself as they exited the stage. Whatever smile he'd put on had apparently only been for the benefit of the assembly.

"Come on, Cinderella. The ball's over and the clock is about to strike midnight."

"Oh, loosen up a little bit, why don't you?" she retorted. She'd been about to end her statement by calling him Prince Charming, but the guy was as far from charming at that moment as anyone could get. He was more like the clock tower, ticking away the minutes in anticipation of ruining the fun. Or maybe one of those carriage attendants who turned back into a mouse at the end of the night.

A big, plump gray mouse with a cowboy hat, enormous pink ears too large for his head and a big black wiggly nose. She chuckled at the thought.

"What's so funny?" he demanded, tossing the rope back to Alexis as he took the steps off the platform two at a time. He threaded his fingers through his thick black hair before replacing his Stetson.

She followed him down the stairs. She imagined he wouldn't appreciate being compared to a mouse, even one in a cowboy hat, so she made a different observation out loud.

"You could use a haircut. Did you know I'm a certified cosmetologist?"

"A cosmo-*what*?" His gaze widened on her, looking as appalled as if she'd just threatened to shave his head. He yanked the rim of his hat down lower over his eyes. "No, ma'am. Not gonna happen. I don't care how much money you paid out for me back there. I'm drawing the line."

Something in the way he said it stirred a challenge in Viv's chest. He had no idea how nice he'd look if he'd give her the opportunity, and she was certain he would.

If he wanted a challenge, she would give him a challenge. She had her ways.

But she pushed the thought away. Cleaning him up wasn't her goal, now that she'd won him. He could look like a bear all he wanted as long as he helped her build her salon. But she doubted that would be any comfort to him. Based on his reaction to even the suggestion of a haircut, she had a feeling he wasn't much of a fan of beauty salons. And that meant he wasn't going to like the project she was about to lay out for him one bit.

If Vivian Grainger thought for one second she was getting anywhere near him with a pair of shears, she was sadly mistaken. Nick liked his hair just the way it was, thank you very much. And even if he did decide to get a trim, he'd see a male barber, not a ditzy, beautiful blonde with a sharp pair of scissors.

Of course the old barbershop in town had closed two years ago when Old Man Baranski kicked the bucket. No one had stepped in to take his place, and the building had eventually been used by Emerson's Hardware for their overstock. Now he had to drive for an hour just to get his hair cut—which is why he didn't bother.

One of the reasons, anyway. If he had a special lady in his life, he might care more about how he looked. But that wasn't the case right now—and it looked like it wouldn't be for a good long while.

He supposed he ought to be grateful to Vivian for bidding on him. After his last—and very public—painful breakup, most of the town's single ladies were avoiding him like the plague, as evidenced by the auction today. He supposed he wasn't really all that surprised no one else bid on him.

Vivian hadn't been back in Serendipity long enough to hear the latest rumors. She'd spent the last few years in Houston and wore Big City like a neon sign around her neck. He wasn't sure getting picked up by a woman like her was going to do his reputation any good, but it couldn't get any worse.

He'd really hoped to be bid on by some little old lady who needed help with a few odd jobs. He'd also been more than a little concerned that an ex-girlfriend with a grudge might see this as an opportunity to repay him for real or imagined wrongs.

He was the first to admit that his record with long-term relationships was less than stellar, and he knew it was his fault. He was just really, *really* not good at making things work in the dating department.

But circumstances being what they were, he might as well see what Vivian wanted and be done with it—as long as it didn't involve cutting his hair. Who knew? Maybe he could mend some of those torn fences with his reputation if folks in town saw that he treated Vivian right.

Nick turned his attention to her, but he stood for a good five minutes while Vivian talked to her sister.

And talked. And talked.

His stomach growled, but he couldn't do anything about it. This was a Bachelors and *Baskets* auction, with the winning bidders providing a picnic lunch for the men they'd won. Lunch wasn't going to happen until Vivian led him to wherever she'd stashed her basket. He had to wait until she decided to grace him with her attention, which he guessed wasn't going to happen soon, since her mind seemed to be on Alexis, the auction and anyone in speaking distance of her.

Except for him.

Vivian gave a new meaning to the words *social butterfly*, and she definitely had the gift of gab. With the possible exception of Jo Spencer, who owned Cup O' Jo's Café and was therefore the Queen of the Gossip Hive, Nick had never seen anybody flitter around as much as Vivian. Her high, tinkling giggle reminded Nick of a fairy in a cartoon.

It was downright grating on his nerves and was practically curling the hair on his chest. Nick crossed his arms and grumbled under his breath, berating the entire chain of events that had led him to this particularly annoying set of circumstances.

She was supposed to be *feeding* him. That was the deal. She had the picnic basket.

Somewhere.

If she ever got around to acknowledging him again, he might ask where it was. He didn't mind eating alone and leaving her to her myriad conversations.

"Hey, Viv," Alexis called, nudging her sister's shoulder. When Vivian turned, Alexis gestured toward Nick. "You need to feed your man. He looks ravenous over there."

Nick bristled. While he appreciated Alexis's thoughtfulness, he was *not* Vivian's man. Not in any way, shape or form.

Except, unfortunately, that in a way he was. She'd bought him. With money. For a purpose as yet unknown to him. Unfortunately, she was very possibly expecting a date out of this. He knew perfectly well that many of the single ladies in the crowd were bidding on men for just such a reason. It was enough to make a single man shudder.

"Oh, Nick, I am so sorry," Viv apologized, laying a familiar hand on his forearm. "I completely forgot about you."

"Yeah. No kidding." His arm trembled as he fought the urge to jerk it out of her reach.

She'd *forgotten* about him? *Ouch.* He didn't want to admit it, but her words stung his ego. Even if it was Vivian Grainger. Even if he shouldn't really care whether she was thinking about him or not.

She ignored his attitude, if she even noticed it, apparently choosing to take the high road and stay cheerful instead of descending into bickering. Typical of what he knew of Vivian Grainger—her glass was always, annoyingly, half-full.

"I packed my basket with all kinds of goodies," she informed him. "Turkey and Swiss sandwiches and BLTs. Potato chips, a couple of deli salads and one of Phoebe's delicious cherry pies for dessert. I hope you like cherry."

Cherry happened to be his favorite. But as hungry as he was, he would have eaten it even if he didn't care for it.

"And I packed a special surprise."

In general, he didn't like surprises—but this one sounded like it was something to eat. His mouth watered at the possibilities.

"You'll be happy to know that everything I've packed today is legitimately store-bought," she continued, without letting him get a word in edgewise, were he inclined to do so.

Which he wasn't.

"I know the whole point of this was to serve the best of Serendipity's down-home country cooking, but trust me when I say you would definitely not want to eat *my* cooking. I can't even boil soup."

"Water," he corrected absently, wondering when, if ever, they were going to get around to actually *eating* the food she was yammering about.

"What?" she asked, confused. She folded her arms over her stomach and swayed slightly, as if she was unsteady on her feet. Instinctively, he pressed a palm to the small of her back to support her.

"Water," he clarified. "The saying is, 'You can't boil water.'"

"Oh." She straightened her shoulders and waved him off, seeming to recover from the dizziness that had come over her moments before. "Whatever. But I do have bottled water." She paused, giggling. "To drink. Not to boil."

He was having trouble following her train of thought, if there was one. Once again he thought of a butterfly, flittering from flower to flower.

Only this particular flying insect was revved up on caffeine or something.

"And your basket is—where?" he finally asked, hoping for a straight answer but not really expecting one.

To his astonishment, she grabbed his hand and tugged him across the green.

"We're right in the middle."

Smack in the middle of the chaos. Now, why was he not surprised?

"It's not that I've never cooked before," she said earnestly, as if she thought he really wanted to know, while spreading a fuzzy purple blanket on the plush green lawn and flopping down on it. She reached into her ribbon-and-plume-decorated picnic basket, which Nick thought resembled an exotic bird, and withdrew two sandwiches. Her gaze turned distant and her lips bowed into a frown. "It's just that I'm not very good at it. Let's just say the whole experiment was a failure."

She paused and her voice made a distressed hiccupping sound. In one blink of an eye her expression filled with deep sadness.

Nick's gut clenched and his natural protective male instinct started blaring five alarms.

Her response seemed a bit of an overreaction for a burned roast or whatever she'd had. What could have possibly happened to make her that upset? Had someone yelled at her? Hurt her feelings? If so, that hardly seemed fair. Cooking wasn't everyone's forte.

His instinct was to probe further, but then, just as quickly as the pain in her eyes had appeared, it was gone. She shook her head and cheerfully went on as if she'd never faltered.

"Would you like turkey and Swiss or BLT?" She punctuated the question with a laugh that wasn't really a laugh.

She held out both sandwiches to him and he gratefully accepted a turkey and Swiss, which was tightly wrapped in cellophane and marked Sam's Grocery. She unwrapped her own sandwich, shook two packets of mayonnaise and globbed it onto her BLT.

"A little sandwich with your mayo?" he teased between bites of his own meal.

She grinned. There was a lot of sunshine in that smile, so much so that it occurred to Nick that he ought to be wearing aviator shades.

"How sad the world would be without

mayonnaise." The black clouds of her past had definitely lifted and her disposition could easily have rivaled Mary Poppins and her spoonful of sugar.

It was hard to keep up with her.

Her eyes glowed with excitement as she reached back into the basket. "Ready to see your surprise?"

He nodded in anticipation, hoping it was food and not tickets to the opera.

He nearly cheered when she pulled out a bucket of hot wings. He was sure he was gaping. How could she possibly have known they were his favorite? What kind of a coincidence was that? The deli counter in Sam's Grocery only carried hot wings on special occasions and they sold out fast. She would have had to put her order in early to get this batch.

"How—how did you guess?" he stammered.

She wriggled her fingers at him and spoke in a Dracula voice. "I r-r-read your mind."

"You sure did," he agreed, reaching for a hot wing. "Or my belly."

"If you want the truth, after I decided you were the guy I was going to bid on, I called your mother."

"You did *what*?" He choked on the hot

wing and nearly spit it out. He didn't know if he was more shocked that she'd planned in advance to bid on him or that she'd been in contact with his mom.

"To find out what your favorite food was. I figured that was the least I could do. Alice was very helpful."

He groaned and swallowed. He could only imagine just how *helpful* his mother had been. Next thing he knew, his mom would be inviting Vivian over for dessert and toting out the baby pictures.

He felt a slight guilty twinge for thinking like that. Ever since his dad had died, it had been a struggle to get their mom to show enthusiasm about much of anything. He should be glad that Vivian's call seemed to have sparked some of that old matchmaking excitement in her. Yet that didn't make the thought of anyone pushing him and Vivian together any less off-putting. He decided to put aside his worries for now and focus on the food. Buffalo wings were too delicious to be spoiled by aggravation or dread.

"Mmm," he groaned. "Best Buffalo wings I've ever had. Bar none."

"I've never really understood that part," Vivian admitted. She'd taken a piece of chicken for herself, but took little more than a nibble before putting it back on her plate. "Buffalo don't have wings. And anyways, I don't think I'd like to eat a buffalo."

Nick barked out a laugh. Somehow taking a detour through Viv's head and picturing buffalo with wings lightened his heart more than anything else in—well, ages.

He reached for another chicken wing. While he polished off several hot wings, two sandwiches and the deli salads, Viv talked. Apparently she didn't need much feedback other than the occasional grunt or nod from him, which was a good thing, since his mouth was always full of food.

Vivian, on the other hand, hardly touched the food on her plate. She'd nibble here and there on her mayonnaise-laden sandwich and then her expression would turn a little green in the gills and she'd put it down again. He wondered if maybe she wasn't feeling well.

He was just about to ask when he stopped himself short, deciding it was none of his business. Maybe it was just his imagination and she always ate like a rabbit. She certainly had the figure for it. It would be rude of him to ask. Besides, whatever was bothering her, it wasn't affecting her soliloquy.

She told him about attending cosmetology school in Houston, how much she loved her work and the city and how her brother-in-law, Alexis's husband, Griff, had helped her finance her first salon and spa. Apparently it had been quite successful, to hear her tell it, at least until the economy tanked. Then everyone's business had taken a big hit.

"So what brought you back to Serendipity?" he asked, wiping his hands on a paper towel. Clearly she liked living in the city well enough and it sounded as if the business world was finally recovering from the economic downturn. "Or are you just visiting?"

Nick was positive he saw her blanch, and then her cheeks turned as red as the cherries in the slice of pie he was about to wolf down.

"I'm here for the long tow," she said with a sigh.

He knew what she meant.

Her blond eyebrows lowered. "I sold my spa in Houston and bought a little shop here in town." She gave a self-deprecating laugh. "I guess you could say that I'm downsizing."

"Why?"

"If you don't mind, I'd rather not talk about it."

Nick tried to catch her gaze but she wouldn't

quite look at him. Here was a woman who normally couldn't *stop* talking. He'd clearly hit on a nerve. And she sounded so *sad*. It hit him right in the gut.

He rapidly backtracked out of the territory that made her uncomfortable. Anyway, he didn't want to know the specifics. It wasn't as if they were going to start hanging out together. Since he was stuck with her until he finished whatever task she had for him, he'd rather deal with the happy social butterfly, if given the choice, for as long as he had to be around her, even if her perky personality drove him half-crazy. These bipolar emotions of hers were creeping him out.

What he needed to do was focus on whatever she required of him. Clearly she had a reason for buying him, or she wouldn't have approached his mother. And he suddenly realized that whatever it was she wanted from him hadn't been addressed at all. It was the only thing she *hadn't* talked about.

It probably had something to do with the shop she'd just bought. Hopefully she was just looking for a little remodeling help or something.

He hoped. That would be safe territory.

And happily, nothing to do with dating. Even if his poor mother hoped otherwise.

Sorry, Mom.

"Where is the building located where you plan to build your new spa?"

For some reason he had trouble with the word *spa* leaving his lips. One little syllable and his tongue was tripping all over it. He supposed it was because he was picturing snowy white bathrobes and massages and people laying out in the sunshine with cucumbers over their eyes.

A spa in Serendipity?

The town had one grocery store. One café. What would it do with a *spa*?

"Two doors east of Emerson's Hardware," she answered, excitement seeping into her voice. "The red building. It used to be a barbershop, but it's been vacant for a while, I think. I imagine it's going to take a little work to get it back into usable condition."

"A *little* work?" he asked, unable to smother an amused grin. Had she even seen the building since she'd bought it? "Lady, Emerson's has been using the building as extra storage space for their feed. I doubt very much they worried about keeping up with internal appearances. And you're looking to make it into some kind of fancy spa?"

"A beauty salon and spa isn't that big of a stretch from a barbershop."

Only night and day.

He snorted. It might have the plumbing and wiring setup she needed, but the interior was going to need a complete redesign—and that was *after* she cleaned out the mess that came from two years of being used as a storage facility. "It's not going to take *some* work. We're talking about a pretty major overhaul here. You're going to have to gut the whole thing out and start from scratch."

She tilted her chin up and smiled at him with a twinkle in her eye. His throat tightened. They might be as different as a tomcat and a spaniel, but he was a guy and she was an extraordinarily pretty woman, whether or not a man preferred blondes. And he'd always been partial to blondes.

"You mean *you're* going to have to gut it," she corrected, a giggle escaping from between her lips. Her impossibly blue eyes were alight with mischief. "That's why I bought you. So I guess now my spa is your... challenge." She reached over and playfully tipped his hat down over his eyes.

"And mine," she continued, as usual not letting him get a word in edgewise, "is going to be trying to work with you every day without coming after you with a pair of scissors in order to trim that thick dark bird's nest of yours."

He pushed his hat back up and grinned. "You can try, lady. You can try."

Chapter Two

From the first second Jo had pounded the gavel and declared that Nick was sold to Viv, she'd been wondering if she had made an enormous mistake in bidding on him.

Now she was sure of it.

For one thing, Nick had stopped eating when she'd told him her plans, a chicken wing halfway to his lips. He'd actually had the nerve to gape at her like she was crazy—and then he'd practically laughed her off the community green for making the choice to buy the little barbershop. He hadn't even bothered to ask if she had good reasons for it.

Which she did.

"We can start work as soon as you're ready," she told him, hoping for sooner rather than later. "I don't know how much time you're willing to give me on this project, but I'll take whatever you offer. I'm anticipating maybe together we can do it in—what? A week? Two weeks?"

The expression that crossed his face was indescribable. The closest thing she could come up with was that he looked like he'd just swallowed a toad. His mouth moved but no words came out.

"What?" she asked, her guard rising. "Did I grow an extra eyeball on my chin?"

His lips twitched. "The expression is 'forehead.'"

She ignored him. "Do you have a problem with my—*our*—new endeavor?"

He groaned and polished off the chicken wing he'd been holding, tossing it into the bucket of empty bones. He'd eaten half the bucket when she'd first offered it to him and was now finishing it off, and that was after having eaten a full lunch and an enormous slice of pie. Hot wings as an after-dessert snack was just plain weird, as was the fact that he'd polished off almost the entire bucket of chicken literally on his own.

And he thought *she* was crazy? *Whatever.*

In contrast to Nick, she hadn't eaten much at all. Her morning sickness was catching up with her. She'd thought she was over the worst of it, but she suspected her nerves weren't helping.

"Do I—er, *we*—have problems? Where do I begin?" he asked sardonically.

"Is this too big of a challenge for you? Because if it is, tell me now. There are a few men left on the auction docket I can bid on if you think this project is more than you can handle."

He snorted. "I can handle it."

She narrowed her gaze. She'd pricked at his ego on purpose to see what he'd do. But it wasn't an idle threat. As far as she was concerned, if he was going to be a jerk to her, she'd follow through with her words and toss him out on his elbow.

She'd had just about enough of dealing with thickheaded men, and she definitely didn't need his guff. She was resourceful and could always figure out another way to renovate her spa. With or without Nick McKenna. Worst-case scenario, she would hire a general contractor. Better than putting up with Nick's less-than-stellar attitude. Talk about a glass-half-empty kind of guy.

"If you can handle the job, then what's the problem?" she jabbed.

He wiped his sleeve across his chin.

Neanderthal.

"I'm not the one with the problem, lady, because I'm not the one who picked up a piece of property that's bound to be more trouble than it's worth. Remodel it in a week? Yeah, not so much."

"You don't know that for sure." Though she had a sinking feeling that he knew more about it than she did. Was one week a totally crazy estimate? She honestly had no idea how long these things usually took.

Heat rose to her face. He must think she was a complete idiot. She wasn't—more like a wishful thinker. Her tendency toward always believing in the best-case scenario had gotten her into trouble more times than she could count, but Nick didn't need to know that.

"No. I don't." He shook his head, his brow lowering. "But I can make an educated guess. Did you buy the shop at below market price?"

Now, how had he guessed that? Alexis and Griff were the only ones who knew the details of her own private financial affairs.

"I might have," she hedged.

He chuckled. "I'll take that as a yes."

"So it's not in as good a shape as it could

be. What does that matter? When it's finished, it'll be amazing. You'll see. I have an exciting vision for it."

She'd made her decision the moment she'd seen the cute little red storefront standing empty in the middle of Main Street, especially when she'd noticed that it used to be a barbershop, no less, right down to the now-cracked twirling peppermint sign. It was locked so she hadn't gone in, and the windows had been too dusty to see much more than shadows inside, but she was sure she could make it into something amazing. She didn't care that it needed work. She'd made the right decision, and now she would stand by it.

Yes, the once-red exterior paint was peeling and the sign hanging from the outside eaves was dangling by a mere thread, but that would have had to have been replaced anyway, with a bright yellow sign declaring her new spa was open for business. When she was finished remodeling, it would be the most sparkling, eye-catching property in all of Serendipity. She'd have customers lined out the door, all excited to take advantage of her many services.

For the ladies of Serendipity, the blessing

of being able to pamper themselves without the hassle of a long drive to the nearest city would finally have come. Full hair services and mani/pedi's. Eventually she hoped to be able to hire a licensed masseuse so she could add massage to her list of services.

And it was *her* special blessing as well, her opportunity to prove herself, to turn her life around and make her world right again.

Her life—and her precious baby's. She needed to be able to provide for her child, but it was more than that. She wanted her son or daughter to have a mother he or she could be proud of.

"Does your vision for this building include having to gut the whole interior before you can rebuild? I'll have to take a closer look at it, but I'm guessing that's what we're going to be looking at."

Her dreams hadn't been overly realistic, she realized, but she wasn't going to admit that. Not to Nick. It was just a slight hiccup in the big scheme of things. She wasn't going to let that stop her.

"I'm not afraid of a little hard work."

He leaned back on his hands and raised an eyebrow. "You know anything about carpentry?"

She shook her head. "Well, no. Not really. But I'm sure I can measure wood and hammer a nail as well as the next woman. And I'm a fast learner. Besides, that's why I brought you in. Or *bought* you in." She giggled at her own joke.

He snorted and rolled his eyes.

"I asked around town who might know a little bit about carpentry and your name came up once or twice. That's why you were on my short list."

"Well, that explains it, then," he remarked cryptically.

"Explains what?"

He shrugged. "I was just wondering why you bid on me. Now I know. And you're right. I know how to help you out. After my dad got sick, I remodeled my mom's ranch house, where all three of us boys were raised. It gave me something positive to do with my anxiety and grief. And once I was done with that, I built cabins for Jax and me from the ground up."

"See, I was right about you. An amateur expert. Or is that an expert amateur?" Vivian smiled and breathed a sigh of relief. With the way Nick had been hedging, for a moment there she thought maybe his skills had

been overrated. She really did need someone who knew what he was doing, and Nick
was that man.

He didn't look convinced.

Why didn't he look convinced?

He'd just told her he'd made a bunch of
stuff, some buildings from the ground up.
Remodeling her shop would be a piece of
pie next to that. Surely he wasn't second-
guessing himself?

She stared at him a moment longer and
then he shifted his gaze away from her and
went foraging into the picnic basket as if it
were a bottomless well of food.

He couldn't possibly still be hungry. He'd
eaten—

Oh.

The lightbulb in her brain flipped on at
the very same moment she took a sucker
punch to her gut. He was avoiding eye contact while he tried to think of how to phrase
the bad news.

It wasn't that he *couldn't* build stuff. He
just didn't want to build stuff for *her.*

He might as well have taken a baseball bat
to her fragile self-esteem. With the help of a
therapist she was slowly crawling out of the
tortuous abyss of being engaged to a verbally

and emotionally abusive man. Derrick had fooled a lot of people with his public persona. His former best friend, Griff. Alexis.

And Viv most of all.

With Derrick, she'd always believed she wasn't good enough for him. She'd tried to change to please him, to be what he wanted her to be, until she didn't even recognize the woman in the mirror. But no matter what she did or didn't do, it was never good enough for him. And when she'd discovered she was pregnant—

No. She wasn't going to go there. Not right now. Derrick wasn't the man she had to deal with right now—Nick was. He may not be the kindest or most tactful man, but she knew he was a good, decent person. He wouldn't attack her deliberately. If anything, he probably thought he was helping her by pointing out the flaws in her plan. He didn't know how much it hurt her to hear her ideas—her dreams, her hopes for the future—put down again. But no matter. If Nick didn't want to help her, he just had to say so. If he was having second thoughts about doing the work, she'd even give him the out he needed, since he hadn't made the most of the first one she'd offered.

"Just forget about it."

His head jerked up. "What did you say?"

"I said forget about it. You don't have to give me a hand with my remodel if you don't want to. I'll find someone else. Worst-case scenario I'll have to hire a contractor. No big deal."

"But the money for the auction—"

"—went to a good cause. No hard feelings."

She didn't want to be here at the auction anymore, hanging out on the community green with most of the rest of the population of Serendipity. She didn't want to sit across from Nick acting like everything was okay when it wasn't. She was tired of pretending.

She reached for the empty sandwich wrappers, stuffed them into the picnic basket and then slammed the lid closed. As closed as her heart felt right then.

She wasn't lying when she said she would make it. Somehow, some way, she would. With or without Nick McKenna's help. She shoved her hand forward, ready to shake his and be done with all of this.

Be done with him.

He frowned and stared at her palm as if it were an overgrown thornbush.

"Now, wait a minute," he said in a gentler tone of voice. Instead of shaking her hand, he laid his large palm over hers and held it. "Don't jump to conclusions. I never said I wasn't going to help you."

She sighed. "You didn't have to say it out loud. It's written all over your face, not to mention in your attitude. I know you think I'm a dumb blonde who couldn't find her way out of a plastic bag, but even I can take a hint."

He threw back his head and laughed. "Paper sack."

"What?"

He just smiled and shook his head. "I'm thick as a tree trunk sometimes. And I know exactly what my mama would say about that kind of stubbornness."

"Yeah? And what's that?" She couldn't help it. She was intrigued.

He twisted his free arm behind his back as if someone in authority were holding it there.

"She'd say," he responded with a grin, "that I need an attitude adjustment." He paused and flashed her a truly genuine smile. "And you know what, Viv?"

"What?" Despite everything, his smile

lightened her mood. Maybe because he only smiled when he meant it.

"My mom would be right."

He snorted and shook his head. "And, Viv? I don't like to hear you beat yourself up. I don't think you're dumb—and you shouldn't let anyone else tell you that, either. Besides, I don't let anyone talk about me that way, and we're in this project together now." This time, he held out his hand, and she couldn't help grinning back as she gave it a shake.

Two weeks following the Saturday of the auction found Nick standing next to Vivian in front of her property. He had tied up all the loose ends that would keep him from his commitment and wanted to get started on this project as soon as possible. Construction was already beginning on the senior center and he planned to volunteer as many hours to that as he could, especially since his uncle James would soon be a resident.

Just thinking of his uncle, an eighty-eight-year-old man with late-stage dementia, was an added weight on Nick's already burdened heart.

His plate was full to overflowing, but he wouldn't allow himself to complain. Ranch work kept him plenty busy on its own, and he couldn't count on his brother Jax to lend a hand as much anymore, since Jax's miserable harpy of an ex-wife had come to town the day of the auction and abandoned month-old twin babies on his doorstep. The baby girls were adorable and an absolute blessing through and through—but that didn't stop them from being a lot of work. With the hours they kept Jax up every night, it was a struggle for him to get through his own horse training work every day, much less help with the ranching responsibilities. Slade had his family and his work at the sheriff's department to keep him busy. So that meant it all fell to Nick.

With everything going on, his stress level was off the scale. The sooner he remodeled Viv's quaint little beauty parlor, the sooner he could get out from under his obligation to her and go back to his primary concerns—his family, the ranch and the senior center.

He and Viv were both gazing up at the weathered wooden sign hanging directly over them from the eaves over the sidewalk. It was barely dangling by a thread. The thing was downright dangerous. He was surprised a good Texas wind hadn't blown it off by now.

He pulled out the pencil he'd tucked behind his ear to scribble a few notes on his clipboard. The hazardous sign was the first item on what he imagined was going to be a very long list of things to do to get this place in working order. He couldn't even imagine what the interior of the building held in store for him.

"I didn't bring a ladder," he said, his free hand resting on his tool belt. He'd known he'd eventually have to bring a truck full of heavy-duty tools to remodel this joint—from a planer to a circular saw and everything in between, but he figured evaluating the work and making a plan of action came first. "We've got to get that sign down. Today, if possible."

He still had no idea what he was getting into, but he figured he ought to at least give Vivian her money's worth in knowledge and labor. The outside of the place only needed a fresh coat of paint and it would be good to go, but he suspected that wouldn't be true of the interior.

"I noticed the sign the first day I was here. I know it's a potential hazard to people walking underneath. I can't imagine why it hasn't been removed before now."

"Nor I," Nick agreed. "You'd think the town council would be on top of something like that. They probably just overlooked it. No matter. You'll need to hang a new sign anyway. What are you going to call the place?"

Vivian propped her fists on her hips and screwed up her mouth, chewing on her bottom lip. She stared at the old sign as if it was going to give her guidance.

"To be honest, I don't know. I'm sure something will come to me once I get more of a feel for the place. It has to be exactly right."

"What did you call your spa in Houston?"

"Viv's Vitality."

"That's clever. You could use that."

She blanched and shook her head.

"No," she stated emphatically. "No. I absolutely couldn't do that. The salon in Houston is part of my old life. This has to be completely different, in every way."

He lifted his hand as if toasting her with a glass of bubbly. "Here's to new beginnings, then."

Her breath came out in an audible sigh. "Right. To new beginnings."

"Let's take a look inside and then I'll run

over to Emerson's and see if they'll let me borrow a ladder."

That was one of the many benefits of small-town living. Nick had gone to school with Eddie Emerson, who would one day inherit his father's hardware shop. Since he'd known Eddie and his father all his life, he was sure it would be no problem to use one of their ladders to take down that sign.

Vivian shoved her hand into an enormously oversize pink-polka-dot handbag that sported a bow nearly as large as the bag itself. At least a good minute of fruitless searching went by before she smiled and shrugged apologetically before returning to digging. He was certain she'd forgotten the keys, but she determinedly continued to fish for them. "They're in here somewhere."

He smothered a grin. What could she possibly need to carry around with her that warranted such a big handbag?

"Ah! Here we are," she announced triumphantly, waving her keys in the air like a flag. She sorted through a large mess of keys until she came upon the one she wanted, and then approached the door.

Nick stepped around her and reached for the key.

"Here. Let me," he said, sliding it into the lock and stepping back, gesturing for her to enter first. "Welcome to your new home away from home."

He blinked hard.

His new home away from home? More like his new *nightmare*.

He'd imagined the interior would take some work—okay, a *lot* of work—but this was even worse than he'd anticipated. There was nothing salvageable that he could see. At best the paint was peeling off the walls, and that didn't count the numerous scratches and holes. Repainting wouldn't be nearly good enough. They'd need all new drywall.

The ground was covered with rotting floorboards scattered with a huge amount of old junk. Besides ancient piles of feed, there was a rusty tricycle, an old end table that appeared to be cracked through the middle, random bricks and an ugly garden gnome that stared back at him as if he were the intruder.

It would take them a week working full-time just to clear the debris, never mind prepare the inside for remodeling. He hadn't committed to this kind of labor.

But he was all-in now. And maybe that

was for the best—at least for his social standing. Vivian knew nothing of his recent dating history, so she didn't know that he was practically a pariah thanks to his vicious ex poisoning everyone against him. But Vivian had always been well liked. If he spent time with her, helping her, making sure he was seen with her, it was bound to give his reputation an upswing. It would show the rest of the town that he could be near a woman without having her run screaming in the other direction.

Or even worse, be screaming *at* him.

In public.

It wasn't that he had any romantic intentions toward Viv, but he had to start somewhere in polishing up his public image if he ever wanted to get a date again. Besides, this project wouldn't last forever. It would be a race to see whether he could finish the project before Vivian discovered the truth about him. His most recent pathetic excuse for a relationship wasn't exactly a state secret, and he was sure Viv had plenty of friends who would be anxious to tell her the whole story.

Anyway, who else would help Vivian with this disaster of a shop if not he? She wouldn't have bid on him if she had anywhere else to go, or anyone else to lean on. He suspected she hadn't had enough money to hire a proper contractor, although she hadn't said as much.

He didn't blame her for her pride. In fact, he admired her for it.

Yes, he had a cattle ranch to run, but he'd figure out some way to be there for Vivian. She was probably only now realizing how long it would take to remodel, but he'd get it done for her.

And run the ranch. And help Jax. And volunteer to help build the senior center.

First, though, he'd have to dig through all this trash.

"Oh, my," Vivian breathed from behind his left shoulder. "This is truly awful."

"You haven't been inside before today?"

Her face colored, staining her cheeks an alluring soft pink. "Honestly? No. The entire real estate transaction was done over the phone and on the internet. I haven't been back in town for more than a couple of days, and I've been busy moving myself into a cabin on Redemption Ranch. Before I knew it, the day of the auction crept up on me, and at that point, I figured we may as well take a look at it together, so we could start making plans."

"So you bought it sight unseen."

"Well, I saw the exterior, and I remembered the location from when I lived here before. The pictures the real estate agent gave me must have been from when the property was still a working barbershop. I had at least some idea of what I was getting into."

Nick personally thought she had *no* idea what she was getting into. The real estate agent who talked her into buying this property should be shot, taking advantage of Vivian that way. And the worst part was she didn't have the slightest idea that she'd been taken.

Whatever she'd paid for it, it was too much.

Vivian shook her head. "I apologize. This is all my fault. I should have come down and inspected the place before I got you involved."

Nick heard the trip in her voice and realized she must have read the expression on his face. She looked as if she were about to cry. She pressed her lips tightly together as if trying to stem the tide of her emotions, which ebbed and flowed faster than Nick could keep up with.

But he could relate to her discouragement. On the work front, he'd recently lost several head of cattle to disease. Then there was his public breakup with Brittany.

Life threw everyone curves. It was how a man—or a woman—responded to those setbacks that showed what kind of person they were.

"Well, I suppose I should call for a Dumpster to be brought in so I can start cleaning," Viv said, wiping her palms across the denim of her blue jeans. "I'll put all the trash in one corner until I can remove it. Do you want to go see about that ladder?"

Nick's gaze widened. He had to admit he'd fully expected her to turn tail and run. But she was just buckling down and pushing forward. Which either made her very brave or completely nuts. At this point he wasn't sure which.

At least there was one problem that would be quick and easy to fix. As Nick suspected, Eddie was only too happy to loan him a ladder—on behalf of Emerson's pretty new neighbor, of course. Eddie obviously saw it as an opportunity to ingratiate himself with the lady. Nick didn't know how he felt about that, but he appreciated Eddie lending him a hand when it came to removing the signage—even if it was for ulterior motives.

By the time Nick brought the ladder back to Emerson's and returned to the shop, Vivian had managed to create quite a large pile of debris in one corner.

"Did you see this?" she exclaimed, pointing to a bent-up red tricycle with missing spokes and flat tires. "Who would leave a tricycle in an abandoned shop?" she asked, folding her arms as if she were suddenly cold. "It kind of makes me sad to think about."

"Are you making up stories in your mind about the poor little child who lost his bike?" he guessed.

Count on Vivian to be nostalgic over a rusty piece of metal.

Her eyes widened on him and then she laughed. "Yes, I suppose I am. You must think I'm a real airhead."

"No, I don't," he immediately countered, then cleared his throat.

Heat filled his chest and rose into his neck. That was exactly what he'd been thinking, and honestly, she'd done little to prove otherwise. Still, it seemed to him that she cut herself down a lot, and it gave him cause to wonder why she was so hard on herself.

"Yes, you do," Vivian scoffed. "And I suspect it's going to take some real work on my part to change your opinion of me. You have the Mr. Darcy Syndrome."

He tilted his head at her in confusion. He knew he'd heard the name somewhere, but he hadn't a clue as to where. "The what?"

"Oh, you are *so* busted. He's the hero of *Pride and Prejudice*, which you absolutely should already know. That book was required reading for every tenth-grader at Serendipity High School since the day the school opened."

He grinned. "Are you going to tell Mrs. Keller on me? She still teaches tenth grade English, you know. I *may* have used Cliffs-Notes to get through. I've never been much of a reader, especially not gushy romance." He didn't mention why he didn't care for reading. His dyslexia was a well-kept secret. Only his teachers and family knew about it.

"There's a movie," Vivian suggested with a laugh. "Several of them, in fact."

"Eww. That would be worse than reading the book." Nick cringed. "You'd have to tie me down to the chair to force me to watch that frilly, girly kind of stuff."

"You have *such* a closed mind."

"Opinionated," he countered.

"Stubborn."

"Okay, we can agree on that."

"So you're stubborn and I'm a complete ditz."

Nick's gaze narrowed on her. "You keep saying stuff like that. Sweeping generalizations and insults that don't really apply to you. I don't get it. Why do you do that?"

"I don't know. You tell me. And do you really think the term *ditz* doesn't apply to me? I bought this property sight unseen and then dragged you into the mess."

Nick suspected it wasn't just moving back to Serendipity from Houston that had kept Vivian's mind busy. It sounded like she was getting over some big emotional hurdles, too. But there was no way he was bringing her past or her hurt feelings into the conversation.

"Like you said, it's Main Street. It was a reasonable assumption to make that the property would be in workable condition when you bought it."

"Yes, but I thought I was only going to have to modify it from a barbershop to a salon and spa. I knew I'd have to paint and wallpaper but I didn't expect that I would have to fix a bunch of holes in the walls. Maybe I could just stuff bouquets of fake flowers in the holes and call it art."

She frowned but her eyes were bright and it was clear from her tone that she was making light of the circumstances.

It was more than he would have done under the same conditions. It was more than he *was* doing. He felt frustrated, angry and discouraged for her and her crazy spa idea.

But somehow, he'd fix the problem. Because he was a man, and that's what men did. His family had so many issues he was helpless to resolve: his father's death, his uncle's dementia, Jax's single parenthood. It was almost a relief to face a problem—no matter how large—that he could actually do something to fix.

Chapter Three

It took two weeks putting in every extra hour he had to get the shop cleared of clutter. Finally, Nick was able to start tearing out the old drywall. He wasn't surprised when Vivian showed up to *help*. Right on time, even though technically she had nothing to do at the shop until the construction was farther along.

Just what he needed—Viv underfoot again.

He had—wrongly, apparently—assumed that flighty Viv would quickly lose interest in the day-to-day construction part of the renovation and leave him in peace to finish off the terms of his obligation to her.

That wasn't happening. Instead, she was always hovering over his shoulder like a bumblebee, asking billions of questions

about every little thing and making annoying, if innocent, suggestions on how they—
meaning *he*—might be able to move things
along a little faster.

She was determined to have her spa open
the week before Thanksgiving. Four months
was plenty of time for him to get the remodeling done, even with Viv hovering around,
and even if he was only working the odd
weekend. But Vivian took it all so seriously,
as if the world would end if the shop didn't
open as scheduled.

He wouldn't have admitted it aloud, but
Vivian amused him. She was so certain all
the ladies in Serendipity would be anxious
to avail themselves of her services for family
get-togethers and holiday parties. He didn't
bother telling her that he thought if the ladies
in town had managed up until now without
the use of a beauty parlor, they'd probably
continue to be fine without one.

Today Viv wasn't hovering quite as much
as she was staring at him—or rather, *inspect-
ing* him, assessing him. Every time his gaze
met Viv's, pinpricks of premonition skittered
over his skin, making the hair on the back of
his neck stand on end. He couldn't shake off
the feeling that she was watching him with

more than just an eye toward the carpentry work he was doing.

For some inexplicable reason, she was examining *him*—and he didn't like it one bit. Whenever their gazes met, her impossibly blue eyes would sparkle and her pug little nose would twitch like a kitten's. And she had the oddest expression on her face. He couldn't help but wonder if her twin sister, Alexis, had filled her in on his very public breakup with Brittany.

He waited for her to ask, but she remained silent, which in itself was off the mark for Viv.

He turned his back, making it a point to ignore her as he focused on ripping out large chunks of the wall with a mallet and a crowbar. It felt good to be able to physically take a little bit of his anxiety out on the drywall. And while it was aggravating to have Viv hovering behind his shoulder, there was something pleasant in being around a woman, other than his mother, who didn't treat him like he had the plague.

No single woman in Serendipity wanted anything to do with him. He couldn't entirely blame them for thinking he wasn't much of a boyfriend. He'd owned up to his mistakes, both to Brittany and to God. That hadn't stopped him from getting publically humiliated at last year's New Year's Eve party.

Nick cringed as shame and humiliation burned through him. New Year's Eve the prior year had been the *night that changed everything* for him, not only socially, but emotionally and spiritually, as well.

He had been working overtime at the ranch all week, nursing sick cattle. The night before New Year's Eve, he'd barely turned in for the night when his mother called. His father had only been gone for a few months and she was having a rough time emotionally. She asked if he could come and sit with her for a while.

He'd ended up staying with her long into the night, keeping her company as she grieved through her first set of holidays without her husband, Jenson. She'd talked for a long time, sharing her memories of Christmases past.

Nick had quietly held her, but it was tough for him to listen to her stories, an extra proverbial punch in the gut, because he hadn't been there when his father passed away. He'd been too busy caring for the ranch, resenting Slade and Jax for leaving him with all the work while they took extra trips to San Antonio to be with their ailing dad.

It was a regret he carried in his heart always, so the opportunity to be available to care for his mother when she needed him seemed the very least he could do to try to make things right.

When he'd woken on the morning of New Year's Eve, he'd been bone weary, but ranch work stopped for no man and Nick had worked from before dawn until well after the sun went down.

He was supposed to be slicking up to take Brittany to Serendipity's annual New Year's Eve bash in town. He'd only slouched onto his couch for a second to take a load off his feet and catch his breath. He hadn't even been aware of closing his eyes until three hours later, when he'd awoken with a start from a deep, dreamless sleep. Somehow he'd gone from sitting up to stretched out full-length, facedown on the couch, with one long leg dangling off the end.

He remembered with alarming clarity the full moon streaming through the front window of his small cabin. It had taken him a few seconds just to figure out where he was, and another beat more before the jolt of realization hit him.

He was late to the party.

Way late.

Like missed-the-kiss-at-midnight kind of late.

He'd dressed in his Sunday go-to-meeting clothes as quick as he could and hightailed it to the party, but he knew even then he was too late to make things right. He felt terrible about letting Brittany down—*again*—but not nearly as bad as he felt when she verbally tanned his hide right in front of the entire town.

Part of the problem was that her tongue-lashing tested his pride and ego—she might have been angry with him, and rightly so, but she didn't have to air their dirty laundry in public for everyone to see. Still, once he'd simmered down, the harder blow came when he'd realized she was right.

He *had* let her down. Had neglected her. Had broken trust with her. Enough that the single women in Serendipity as a whole tended to avoid him, and every woman he'd asked for a date since that time had turned him down flat.

A man could get a complex. How was he

supposed to prove that he'd learned his lesson and that he could do better if no one would give him a chance?

And *that* was the real reason he was committed to seeing Vivian's project through to completion, however silly he thought the idea of a salon and spa was on a personal level. To prove to the ladies in town—and, perhaps equally important, to *himself*—that folks could depend on him. That he was trustworthy, and not a total flake.

"How can I help?" Vivian asked, snapping him from his reverie.

"Bring me the push broom, please," he answered without turning to look at her. "It's in the back corner."

The next moment he heard a *thunk*, and then a *crumble* and then a *crash*.

What—?

He whirled to find Vivian sprawled in an inglorious heap in the middle of a pile of old drywall, shrapnel from a damaged ceiling panel snowing down on top of her. Apparently, she'd caught her foot on one of the boards, lost her balance and knocked the broom handle into the ceiling, all in the space of a few seconds.

He tethered his hammer and strode across

the room, his pulse rushing through him. Why on earth had she been standing on top of the drywall? Did she not see the danger there? Couldn't she have taken a less precarious path?

He breathed a sigh of relief when he realized she was fine, though probably a little embarrassed about her trip and fall. She crossed her arms and narrowed her eyes on him, daring him to say something.

Or worse, to laugh, which he was very close to doing, if only because she made an oddly adorable picture all sprawled out on the floor with her legs sticking out like a toddler having a tantrum. When she puckered her lips and blew dust and her bangs off of her forehead, he nearly lost it. Mirth bubbled in his chest.

He reached out both arms in a silent offer to assist her to her feet. He didn't trust himself to speak yet, afraid a chuckle would emerge.

She made an indistinguishable squeak and ignored his outstretched hands, choosing instead to roll to her knees and push to a standing position by herself, only using her palms for support.

Not such a great idea on broken drywall, which immediately cracked through.

She was vertical for about one second before she yelped and nearly crashed back to the floor.

Nick leaped forward, wrapped his arms around her and pulled her into his embrace, her head tucked under his chin and her feet dangling well off the ground as he swung her far away from the hazard. It was a good thing his reflexes had been honed by years of working with horses and cattle, or else Vivian would have landed straight onto her cute little nose.

"Put. Me. Down." Her words were muffled in the cotton of his shirt, but even so, he could tell she was irritated.

With him, apparently.

And here he'd just rescued her. He would have thought she would be grateful.

Women.

She wriggled against him and he opened his arms, relaxing his grip so suddenly that she didn't have time to respond—which served her right for her ingratitude.

He didn't set her down that hard, so he expected her to waver slightly and then right herself, but instead it appeared she was going down again. Her arms flailed in large circles and she squeaked in pain.

This time Nick ignored her protests and scooped her full up into his arms, cushioning her by cradling her against his chest. He stalked to the other side of the room, where he'd set up a metal folding chair he used for snack breaks. He pushed his lunch cooler off the seat with the side of his boot, not caring when it tipped upside down and the lid popped open. His water bottle rolled over his sandwiches, squishing them, but he had other, more important things to worry about.

Like what was really wrong with Vivian. There was more to this than just clumsiness.

He plunked her down into the chair as gently as he could, given the circumstances. She stiffened and glared at him.

Stubborn woman. Would she rather he just tossed her around like a sack of potatoes? He could have thrown her over his shoulder into a fireman's carry and have been done with it. But no. He was trying to be a gentleman here, and she wasn't helping.

Actually, she was tensed on the edge of the seat as if she were listening for the bell that would hurl her out into the boxing ring so she could take a swing at him.

Back when he was with Brittany, they'd had plenty of shouting matches. She hadn't hesitated to pick at him for every flaw and shortcoming, and he'd never been slow to defend himself...at full volume.

He straightened.

Nope. Not this time. He wasn't going to take the bait no matter how much heat was building under his collar. If they started verbally sparring, it was just a matter of time before their disagreement spread around town.

The flittering butterfly thing. It was going to be his downfall.

He couldn't afford another story circulating about his inability to treat a woman properly, even if the only thing he'd done wrong this time was to help her when she didn't want helping.

He was absolutely clueless as to what to do with her, and afraid that whatever he said or did would be the wrong thing.

"What were you thinking?" she demanded, perching one fist on her thigh and shaking a finger at him like he was an errant preschooler.

Her words startled him and he widened his gaze on her, shuffling through his previous thoughts for something that wouldn't stir the flames. "I—er—"

What had *he* done?

"You can't just go around picking people up that way, you big brute."

That was her problem?

"You would have preferred to have fallen?"

"I wasn't going to fall. I just—" she stammered as she searched for words, then harrumphed loudly and fell silent.

Nick lifted a brow and pursed his lips to contain the snicker about to emerge.

Viv wrapped her arms protectively around herself. "Okay. I'll admit I might have been a little off balance. But you were the reason I was about to take another digger in the first place. You set me down off balance on purpose."

He shrugged and grinned, neither assenting to nor denying her accusation. He *had* kind of dropped her. On purpose, although he'd had no intention of making her fall. But it served her right for not recognizing he was trying to help her.

He wouldn't have let her fall.

No—he'd gone and carried her in his arms—quite literally swept her off her feet, and then dumped her into a chair. Now he could see how *that* might come off as manhandling, to the uninitiated.

"I apologize," he said, the corners of his

lips arcing downward. "In my defense, I legitimately thought you might be hurt. You were making all these funny squeaking sounds. Truth be told, I'm surprised you *weren't* injured, between the crumbling ceiling panel and that mess of old drywall."

"Well, as you can see, I am perfectly fine."

He crossed his arms and tilted his head, regarding her closely. She had snowy-white ceiling panel dusting her hair and cascading all down her shoulders, probably ruining her shirt. He wasn't sure why she chose to wear such a nice bright pink blouse when they were doing dirty work, anyway. The woman didn't know the meaning of *dress down*. But even considering all that, he had to admit that from his standpoint, which was admittedly male, she looked mighty *fine*... if you ignored the chunks of ceiling in her hair, that is.

Yet another thought he believed wise to keep to himself. He might be slow on the uptake, but his mama hadn't raised an idiot.

"Now, if you'll—" She stood, squealed in alarm and sat back down again with a thump. Murmuring in pain, she reached for her left foot.

He frowned for real this time and immediately crouched before her, gently taking her foot between his palms.

"I knew it. You *are* hurt." He felt no gratification in being right, or in saying I told you so.

"Did you sprain your ankle when you fell?"

He prodded the area tenderly, feeling for swelling and expecting another painful utterance from Vivian.

She didn't say a thing. Not even a peep. She was too busy gritting her teeth.

"I don't feel any swelling in your ankle." Maybe it wasn't so bad after all, and she'd just mildly twisted it.

"That's because it's not my ankle that hurts," she hissed, squeezing her eyes closed.

He bowed his head and looked closer, but couldn't see anything. "What, then?"

"It's my heel. It feels like I stepped on a long, rusty nail."

Nick swallowed hard. Rusty nails were nothing to play around with, and there were plenty of long, jagged nails where she'd been standing. She'd probably have to get a tetanus shot, and he knew from experience that those things hurt for days.

He checked the bottom of Vivian's sneaker

for a nail and, seeing none, tenderly unlaced her shoe.

He blamed himself for not being more careful. No matter what happened from here on out, he'd be at her side, holding her hand. He could just picture Dr. Delia plunging the needle into her arm. Vivian would be brave, of course, and not want to make a big deal out of it. And every second he was standing there he'd be feeling guilty that he hadn't taken more care with that drywall. He should have given better thought about Vivian's safety.

If she was hurt, it was all his fault. He wished he could take the pain on himself.

As gently as possible, he rolled off her sock, examined her heel and found—*nothing*. No nail mark. No puncture wound. Not even redness or a scrape.

Nothing.

"Give me my sock," she demanded, reaching for it. Nick's immediate and instinctive reaction, no doubt from growing up with a couple of pesky brothers, was to yank it out of her reach.

In hindsight, that was probably not the best idea he'd ever had. She lunged for her sock, missed and ended up sprawled on the floor—

the very thing Nick had been trying to avoid for the last ten minutes.

"I said it *felt* like I had a rusty nail in my foot, not that there actually was one," she snapped crossly, in a deep, husky tone that wasn't anything like her usually high, bird-like tweet.

She must really be in pain, but she was being stubborn about it.

She rolled to a sitting position and grabbed for her sock. This time he let her have it.

"I probably just caught my heel on the edge of a board or something. The soles of these shoes are pretty thin—I'm not surprised I felt it, but as you can see, it didn't do any damage. I'll be fine."

He handed her the sneaker. "Except for the fact that you cannot walk," he pointed out helpfully.

"I'll live," she said through clenched teeth.

He'd never in his life had the misfortune of interacting with as obstinate a woman as Vivian Grainger.

"Be that as it may, you were injured on my watch and I'm taking you to see Dr. Delia."

"No, I—"

He held up his hand, staving off her flood of words. "I insist."

"But it's not necessary—"

"I think it is, and you're going to humor me. The doctor's co-pay will come out of my pocket. I sincerely hope there is nothing wrong with your foot, but I won't rest until I've heard that straight from the doctor's mouth."

Her gaze appeared to be a little bit of deer-caught-in-the-headlights, with a tiny smidge of tiger-in-a-cage added in for good measure.

What was the big deal? She was obviously in pain. Going to see the doctor was just plain sensible. It couldn't be about the money, since he'd already insisted he would pay for the visit. If there was nothing wrong with her foot, then fine, but he felt it was always better to be safe than sorry.

Strange. It almost seemed like Vivian was *afraid* to visit the doctor, even though she'd known Delia for a long time.

Was something else bothering her?

Stubborn, tenacious, bullheaded bear of a man.

Vivian wished with all her heart that she could go back to the day of the auction and bid on someone else—*anyone* else, besides this…this…mulish, dictatorial *hulk*. Someone who wouldn't constantly insist on sticking his head into her business—and now, by extension, into her baby's business.

She sighed and clasped her hands on her lap. She had to concentrate in order to keep herself from her natural maternal instinct, which was to cover her belly with the flat of her palm. That would be a dead giveaway if ever there was one. She refused to look at the giant of a man sitting next to her, whose size dwarfed Dr. Delia's small, pleasantly decorated waiting room. She was glad they were the only ones here to see the doctor.

If Vivian wasn't careful, the truth about her pregnancy was going to come out way sooner than she was ready for it to. She'd hoped, before it became public knowledge, that she'd have a chance to get her spa fixed up and her business started. Then she could at least say she was a woman who'd made mistakes but who had turned her life around rather than what she seemed like now—incapable on every level.

Oh, who was she kidding? She scoffed inwardly. She was never going to be able to keep her secret until after the spa opened—not once she'd realized how much work the building truly needed.

She was nearly five months pregnant and with her normally slender build, it was becoming harder and harder to mask her growing middle section. There was only so much a pair of yoga pants and a billowing blouse could do for a pregnant woman.

Heat rose to her cheeks and she bowed her head in case Nick should see her distress. Would the embarrassment and humiliation never cease?

It wasn't that she didn't love her unborn child—she did, more than she ever thought it was possible to love a person.

But she was so ashamed of herself for how her little one had been conceived. Out of wedlock, and with a man who hadn't loved her. Not only had she set aside everything she believed in and denied her own moral standards, but she had set aside her relationship with God and had given in to the pressure and manipulation of a man who'd turned tail and run at the news that she was pregnant with his child.

And so she had insisted on hiding her pregnancy from the world, even though there was no possible way to continue with the ruse, especially now.

How foolish could a woman be?

She sighed inwardly. What was done was done and there was no turning back the clock. She couldn't change any of it—and she wouldn't want to, if it meant giving up the precious blessing growing inside her. She wanted this baby so much that her heart ached. She'd fallen completely and irrevocably in love with the little sweetheart the first time she'd seen the little bean with a strong, tiny heartbeat thumping on the ultrasound machine screen.

For that beautiful child's sake—and for her own—she was determined to change the vector of her life, embrace the faith she'd once denied, admit her mistakes not only to the Lord and herself, but to the community she lived in, and move on as a single mother.

It wasn't like she was the first woman ever to find herself in such a situation, and it wasn't as if she wouldn't have any help raising her baby. Alexis and Griff would always be there for her and Baby G, the nickname she'd given to her unborn baby in lieu of saying "him or her" all the time. And if family wasn't enough, she had plenty of friends and neighbors in Serendipity, especially within her church community, whom she knew she could count on to help her when she needed it.

Even Nick McKenna.

The thought sprang into her mind right out of nowhere, surprising her with its intensity. She dashed a glance at Nick from underneath her eyelashes.

Strong, steady Nick McKenna, with his back straight, his shoulders set and his large, capable hands clasped in his lap. His head was bowed as if in prayer, but his eyes were open.

He'd been by her side a lot in the last few weeks, supporting her emotionally as much as physically in the labor he was providing for the remodel. He'd brought her to the doctor when he thought she was injured, and had even offered to pay for it, not that she was going to let him.

Given the circumstances, it seemed only right that he be one of the first people to know about the baby and share in her joy. The only people she'd told so far had been her family and Dr. Delia, since she was under Delia's care.

"Nick, I—" she started, and then paused.

His head came up and his striking blue eyes met hers. He smiled softly. "Yeah?"

"I just wanted to tell you—" Vivian tried

again, but at that moment Dr. Delia entered the room.

"What have we got going on here?" Delia asked with a pleasant smile and a nod in both their directions.

Heat suffused Vivian's face and she started to stammer an answer before she realized Delia was asking why she needed to see a doctor and not what might be going on between her and Nick.

Which was nothing.

Nick chuckled under his breath and Vivian wondered if he might have realized where her thoughts had gone, but aloud he said, "Vivian had a bit of a fall at her shop today. Got her foot caught up in some old drywall while we were working on the remodel."

She noticed that he didn't say anything about the broken ceiling panel raining down on her head, which had been entirely her fault. She'd been watching Nick work instead of paying attention to where she was going, and when she'd slipped on the drywall, she'd launched the broom handle straight through the ceiling.

She gasped. Come to think of it, she must look like a complete mess. She dabbed at her face with her palms and they came off covered with white powder.

She did *not* want to see herself in a mirror right now. It was a wonder that Nick and Delia weren't laughing at her awful appearance.

But instead they were completely serious and obviously concerned for her health, although Delia was no doubt alarmed for an entirely different reason than Nick was.

"The bottom of my foot hurts," she hastened to say, to clear the situation up before things got messy.

Delia nodded, but she wasn't looking at Viv's foot. It was Vivian's belly under the doctor's careful scrutiny. Viv didn't know how Nick could *not* notice the direction of the doctor's consideration.

"Nick, do you think you can help her to the examination room?"

For a man Nick's size, he was incredibly gentle in leading her into the examination room. He hovered over her like a mother goose. He even gave her extra support to get onto the table before he returned to the waiting room.

Dr. Delia closed the door, not noticing when it caught on the door jamb and bounced back open a sliver. "I'll take a look at that foot, but since you fell, Viv, we probably ought to have a look at the baby, as well. I'm sure there's nothing wrong, but I believe we should err on the side of safety, just in case."

A deep, audible gasp sounded from the door. Nick stood gaping, clutching her handbag to his chest as if he was experiencing a heart attack.

"Baby?" Nick strode forward and took her elbow. "What baby? I thought you might need your handbag and the door was open a crack so I—a baby?"

Vivian cringed. This was not how it was supposed to go. Sure, she'd been about to tell him the truth about her pregnancy, but she'd wanted it to be on her own terms.

Delia shot Viv a distressed look. "I'm sorry."

Viv laughed shakily. "No worries. It's not common knowledge yet, but it soon will be. It's not like I can keep Baby G a secret for much longer, anyway. The cat is officially out of the sack. It's time to share my good news with everyone."

"What baby?" Nick asked again, staring at Vivian as if she'd grown a second head. In some ways, she had—a tiny one—and a second body, as well. It had been a long day and Vivian was already feeling overwhelmed. She sputtered out a shaky laugh under her breath, mostly from nervousness.

"What is so funny about that?"

Okay, so it was a surprise to him, but he didn't have to act so shocked about it. She was a woman. Women had babies. And what difference did it make to him, anyway?

"I'm pregnant," she said in the voice she'd use when explaining something to a child. Nick was kind of acting like one.

"Since when?"

"Excuse me?" Now Viv was downright offended. What business was it of his when her baby had been conceived?

"I mean, how far along are you?" He huffed impatiently and shoved his hands in his pockets.

"Almost five months now."

He didn't appear scandalized anymore— he looked appalled and slightly horrified. His eyes were huge and brewing a midnight storm.

"You were… And you… And then…" He sputtered to a stop, tapped his cowboy hat against his thigh and threaded his fingers through his thick black hair. He gaped at her midsection. "Oh, man. I can totally see it now. I don't know how I even…"

He appeared to be holding a conversation with himself. Vivian found it a tiny bit amusing, even given the circumstances.

"I can't believe… But of course at the picnic…you were sick to your stomach. I don't know how I didn't realize that you…"

Vivian met Delia's gaze over Nick's shoulder and they exchanged a smile. Throw a baby into the mix and they'd managed to completely confuse the poor, lost male in the room.

"How could you?" Nick's voice had risen as he spoke but now it had dropped onto a cold, icy plain.

How could she get pregnant?

By trusting the wrong man, a man to whom she shouldn't have given her heart. By believing a lie. By letting her faith slide and—

"How could you come into a dangerous construction site with no thought to your safety? You could have been seriously hurt. Your baby—"

Vivian stared at him, her mouth agape. She was having trouble following the conversation, but apparently Nick's concern wasn't how she'd gotten pregnant so much as why she had shown up to help with the construction of her shop.

Well, that was an easy question to answer. Being pregnant was neither here nor there. She wasn't totally incapacitated. Women worked until their ninth month. What century did he think they were living in?

"I was taking ownership," she explained defensively. "I'm not going to leave all the work to you. It's *my* business, after all. At the end of the day, I'm the one responsible for how it turns out. It's my job to oversee the renovation."

Nick snorted and shook his head. "You can supervise from a distance. You don't have to be constantly on-site for that. You're pregnant. Very. Pregnant."

It seemed to Vivian that Nick was blurting out the obvious, and he was repeating himself. But to what end?

To insult her? To get her dander up? Because he was certainly succeeding if that was his aim.

"Yes, well, that much is true," Delia inserted, laying a calming hand on Nick's forearm and herding him toward the doorway. "Which is why I'm going to have to ask you to return to the waiting room. I need to do an ultrasound to check on Baby G. I think we might need to x-ray Viv's foot as well, just to be on the safe side on that issue. We're going to cover all our bases. Do you mind giving us some privacy, Nick?"

Vivian thought that Nick looked like he minded—very much. He paused long enough for her to fear that he'd refuse to leave the room. Thankfully, after a moment, he met her eyes. His gaze slid from there down to her belly before he huffed and puffed and charged out of the room, slamming the door behind him.

"Men, huh?" Delia said with a chuckle as she helped Vivian lie back on the examination table. "You can't live with 'em, can't shoot 'em."

Vivian nodded in agreement. Although frankly, at the moment, shooting Nick didn't seem an entirely unreasonable idea.

"Nick is a good one at heart, though," Delia continued. "He really seems to care for you."

Vivian felt like Delia had shocked her with a cattle prod. The last thing Vivian needed was for Delia or anyone else to get the wrong idea about her relationship with Nick—if one could even call what they had a relationship. It was a business arrangement, nothing more.

"Yeah. About that—" Vivian mumbled, but Delia didn't appear to hear her.

"Let's take a look at Baby G. We might even be able to tell if it's a boy or girl. What do you think, Viv? Do you want to know?"

Vivian sighed. There was a *lot* she wanted to know, and the sex of her baby was only one of many questions she had. She'd never been so confused in her life.

But she could get an answer to *this* question.

She took a deep breath and nodded.

Chapter Four

Despite the way Nick suddenly treated her like she was made of fine china, Vivian and Nick—mostly Nick, to Vivian's exasperation—had spent the next two weekends conquering the enormous pile of debris that was the inside of her shop. Together, they gingerly moved through her building and systematically tossed the rotting wood, broken drywall and most of the eclectic collection of abandoned storage items into a pile outside the back door.

All except the rusty tricycle.

She just couldn't let that one go. The paint was faded and flaking and some of the spokes were bent. The streamers on the handlebars had seen better days and the little bell didn't work at all. A sensible person would recognize it as the junk it was. Vivian knew she ought to toss it, but she couldn't bring herself to do so. She had no idea whether it was even possible to fix the poor, abandoned toy, but she had to try.

For her son.

She laid a hand over her swelling stomach.

Her *son*. She pictured a blond-haired, blue-eyed little boy riding on his restored tricycle, zooming around on the front concreted driveway of a quaint little cottage, pedaling as fast as he could and ringing the bell with wild abandon.

No, she wasn't going to give up on the tricycle, any more than she was going to give up on the pathetic little shop that would take more work than it was probably worth.

And now it was yet another Monday. She considered Mondays a brand-new start of another week, as yet unwritten, and another opportunity to move forward with her life.

As she approached the back entrance to her shop, she was still dwelling on happy thoughts of her baby and his little red trike and she didn't immediately comprehend that something was amiss. But when she reached to put her key in the lock, she realized the door was already open a crack, creaking softly back and forth in the breeze.

Hadn't she locked up when they'd left late Saturday afternoon?

She was fairly certain she had, though her mind had admittedly been full of myriad details regarding what was next on her miles-long to-do list. Had she been so caught up in her thoughts that she forgot to do something that was second nature to her?

Even if it was possible that she'd walked out the door without locking it behind her, she would have closed it, at least. She was one hundred percent certain about that. Who left their door wide-open when they left for the night?

Even a ditzy blonde didn't do that.

A chill rose up her spine. Had someone been in the shop when she wasn't there?

She froze, forgetting to breathe. Could she have been robbed? Had a thief broken in through the back door in order to steal from her?

She clapped a hand over her mouth and snickered at her own silliness.

A *thief*?

She must not be getting enough beauty sleep. Her imagination was running away from her. First of all, she'd be hard-pressed to find any thief within fifty miles of this town. Serendipity's police department hadn't arrested more than an occasional teenage shoplifter in years. Life in the small town was so safe that folks left their houses and cars unlocked and didn't give it a second thought.

Besides, what would anyone want to steal from this broken-down old storefront? There hadn't been anything but garbage to rob before she'd bought the place and there wasn't anything now. Nick hadn't brought in any of his heavy-duty tools yet, and as for his regular tools, he took them with him when he went home for the day. If someone *had* gone to the effort of breaking in, they were welcome to help themselves to the leftover pile of trash.

The answer struck her like lightning.
Nick must have unlocked the door.

He'd probably stopped in to take measurements or something and had forgotten to lock up behind him. She didn't work Sundays, but she knew Nick sometimes did. He was assisting her in addition to the work on his ranch and helping out with the construction of the senior center, so he had to squeeze in time for the shop whenever he could. As a result, she'd given him a key along with full run of her shop, so he could go in and out as he pleased. She was grateful to him for taking on so much extra responsibility—far beyond what her measly three-hundred-dollar auction bid really merited. He still teased her about the concept of opening a spa, but it was good-natured now, and she believed it was just part of his playful nature rather than a dig or criticism aimed at her. And when it came to the work, he never complained, and it looked as if he would be staying until the completion of the remodel.

Come to think of it, she'd have to thank him when she saw him next.

My, how he would laugh when she told him about her encounter with the invisible, imaginary robbers. Another strike against her in the ditzy-blonde category. She even surprised herself sometimes. She chuckled and swung the door open, shaking her head at her folly.

She gasped and stopped cold, a chill running down her spine as she realized that the *nothing* she'd imagined was really *something*.

Just as quickly, the chill passed and fury flared back up in its place, one nerve at a time all the way from the bottoms of her feet to the top of her head. Her breath snagged in her throat and she blinked back the sting of angry tears.

There weren't any thieves in the building, but there was something—two *somethings*, as a matter of fact. And they were making a great deal of noise, not to mention an enormous, smelly mess in a building that was already a walking disaster area to begin with.

Cows.

Two furry black-and-white-spotted baby cows with twitching ears and wet pink noses.

Vivian's thoughts were so clouded that seeing red wasn't just a figure of speech.

Nick.

Was this his sick idea of a joke?

Vivian wasn't laughing.

She didn't pause to consider that it might have been anyone else besides the cynical, blue-eyed cowboy. He was a cattle rancher after all, so he would have no problem getting ahold of a couple of calves. If she wasn't mistaken, that was his ranch's brand. And while he'd been very supportive of her—literally, physically supportive, hovering around her like he thought he'd be needed to prop her up or stop her from falling at any moment ever since he found out about the baby—he'd continued to tease her about her plans to open up a salon and spa in Serendipity.

She had *thought* it had graduated into gentle banter, with no real condemnation behind it anymore. But apparently she'd thought wrong.

And he had a key to the place.

A second ago, before she'd entered the building, that thought had been comforting. Now it was downright infuriating.

She ignored the stab of personal betrayal she felt. She refused to give him the power to hurt her. He didn't get to do that. She would never let a man have power over her in that way ever again.

And here she'd thought he was starting to come around, that he was warming up to her ideas. That he'd actually planned to *help* her get her business up and running. There were moments she'd even believed he was enthused by the project, or at least by the remodeling part of it.

Apparently she'd been wrong. So very wrong.

How *could* he?

How could he possibly imagine that this *prank* was funny, putting two live, dirty, stinking animals inside her shop?

Okay, so privately she had to admit the calves were a teensy bit cute, with their huge, blinking brown eyes, twitching ears and flicking tails. But the stench stung her eyes and she had to cover her nose and mouth just to breathe. She could only be thankful she'd chosen to wear a scarf today.

There were cow patties everywhere she stepped—and she wasn't wearing her riding boots. Why would she be? She hadn't expected to encounter *livestock* today.

She sighed, wondering how long the calves had been there. How could two little cows make so much of a mess? Or had Nick toted in some extra manure just for kicks? She wouldn't put it past him.

Sputtering and grumbling under her breath, she mentally listed all the ways she could calculate Nick's demise. Then she fished her cell phone out of her purse and punched in his number, her poor phone taking the brunt of her anger.

Nick was on speed dial, more's the pity. It was second on the list, right underneath Alexis. His number would be deleted as soon as he came and cleaned up his mess. She pacified herself by imagining how good it would feel to press that delete key and see his scruffy face disappear from her contacts list for good.

Just like *he'd* go away. And she wouldn't be at all sad to see him walk out the door. Or at least not much. There was still a part of her—

"Nick?" she demanded when he picked up on the first ring.

"Viv? What is it?" He managed to sound genuinely concerned, the jerk. "I can tell something's wrong by the tone of your voice."

"Ya think?"

He paused. "Meaning?"

"Meaning this isn't one bit funny." Why was he playing with her emotions? Apparently he had no idea how difficult all this was for her—even without the calves mooing in the background. Did he really think it would be funny to string her out this way?

"If I knew what you were talking about I'd probably agree with you."

"So you know nothing about the cows." It wasn't even close to a question.

"The *cows*?" Nick's query *was* an actual question. He had the nerve to sound flummoxed, as if he really *didn't* know what she was talking about.

"Mmm," she said noncommittally, deciding to let him dig his own grave.

"Viv, what cows?" Now his voice had an edge to it.

"The ones you put in my shop, of course," she said, trying to sound nonchalant about it.

There was silence on the other end of the line for a beat, then two.

"Vivian, are you in the spa building right now?" His voice was a low growl.

"Unfortunately for my sense of smell and my new sneakers, I'm afraid so."

Not that it was a spa yet. Not even close. In fact, with the stench in the room, it was about as far from anything soothing as it was possible to be.

"Stay there. I'll be right over. Better yet, go outside and wait for me. Don't worry, though. Cows are almost always docile animals. They won't hurt you."

"I'm not afraid of them hurting me," she snapped. She was at the end of her string with this man. What kind of an idiot did he think she was? "But I don't want them inside my shop. Nick, they lick their noses."

So gross.

He chuckled. "Yes, I guess they do."

"This is not a laughing matter."

He cleared his throat but she could still

hear traces of amusement in his voice. "No. Of course not. Hang tight. I'll be right there."

Vivian waited impatiently for Nick to arrive, rehearsing in her mind all the things she wanted to say to him. She'd probably get flustered and not manage to say half of what she was thinking now, but she continued to fume and plan her rant anyway.

Given the enormity of the prank, she would have thought he'd be lying in wait, ready to see her immediate reaction to the animals currently lounging in her future place of business. Why had he been sitting at home waiting for the phone to ring? That was weird.

But she supposed he couldn't have known exactly when she'd finish her errands and come by the shop. And besides, his little idea of a joke wasn't going anywhere without his assistance. He had to have known she'd have to call on him to help her get these calves out of her building.

Oh, irony of ironies.

When he arrived less than five minutes later her suspicions reinflated, ballooning to new heights. His house was at least a ten-minute drive away, assuming he drove the speed limit. So maybe he *had* been close—if not watching her, then at the very least hanging out at Cup O' Jo's gleefully waiting for her to call.

As he exited his truck, she planted her hands on her hips and glared at him. He strode forward, lifting his hat and threading his fingers through his thick black hair.

"Where are the cows, then?" he asked without preamble.

As if he didn't know.

She thumbed over her shoulder, pointing to the door of her shop. "In there."

His eyebrows rose to epic heights, as if he still didn't believe what she was telling him. As if he hadn't been the one to plant the black-and-white-spotted bovines there in the first place. He'd missed his calling, being a rancher—he was a much better actor than she'd expected.

She almost believed him.

He entered the shop with Vivian right on his heels. She didn't want to miss any of his forthcoming explanation, which she was certain had to be well rehearsed.

But what if he just laughed at her? After all, this was some kind of cruel prank, aimed at humiliating her.

He took one look at the cows and then spun

around, and ran a hand across his bearded jaw. "Well, they aren't cows."

"What? Of course they're cows. They aren't *horses*, for pity's sake," she pointed out acerbically. "I know what a cow looks like, Nick."

"No, I meant these little heifers aren't even close to being full grown."

She rolled her eyes. "Oh, that makes me feel *so* much better, then. I have two *young* cows standing around in my future spa, blinking their big eyes and chewing their cuds. And making a stinky mess with their cow patties, I might add."

"Yes, I can see that." Humor lined his voice, though she could tell he was trying to temper it.

He seriously thought this was funny. It was all she could do not to punch him in the arm, except that she'd probably end up hurting her knuckles on his mass of muscles.

Thoughtless hulk of a man.

"I don't care what you call them. I want you to get your cows out of here now. And don't bother coming back."

"*My* cows? These aren't—"

He paused, then moved forward to press a

hand against the flank of the nearest heifer, right above the brand.

"I don't—that is—"

"What?" she demanded, crossing her arms and glaring at him. She couldn't *wait* to hear his lame excuse.

"I don't understand." She raised her eyebrows and waited. "You're right. These are my cattle, and this is my brand. The Circle M." He shook his head. "I don't know what to tell you, Viv. I honestly don't know what's going on right now, or how these calves got in here, but you have to believe me when I tell you I didn't do this."

Oh, she *had* to believe him, did she? If he thought that, then he didn't know her very well.

Not well at all.

Nick couldn't believe his eyes. Vivian hadn't been kidding about the live heifers in her shop, however implausible it had seemed when she'd first informed him of it.

Even worse, before she'd even spoken to him about it, she'd been certain that he was to blame. She hadn't given him the benefit of the doubt at all.

How could she even *think* he'd do something like that to her? Even if he didn't care for her, he'd never do anything so hurtful— not when he knew how much the spa meant to her, and how hard she was working to make it a reality.

And the truth was, he *did* like her. They were friends, or at least he'd thought they were. A friend wouldn't accuse another friend of this kind of prank without solid evidence, would she?

He'd thought they'd been getting along fairly well. He was committed to seeing the project through to its conclusion.

And then she'd gone and blamed him for this. She hadn't even asked—she'd assumed. That hardly seemed fair.

Resentment flared in his chest. If she didn't think he was a better man than one who'd do something this hurtful, then it would be better for both of them if she found someone else to do the rest of the labor for her remodel.

Then again…

He took a deep, cleansing breath and attempted to think the situation through rationally. Despite his innocence in the matter, he supposed Vivian had good reasons for suspecting him. The evidence did kind of add up against him.

He had a key to the shop, for one thing. And it was, after all, his brand on the heifers. There was no doubt about it—they were his cattle.

How they'd gotten there was a mystery—one he intended to solve, not only to vindicate himself, but also to find out who had accessed his herd without his permission. And, most of all, to get back into Vivian's good graces, although why he should care was beyond him.

Vivian had told him in no uncertain terms that she didn't want to see him back again, which really battered his ego. She'd shown more tact than Brittany in not yelling at him in front of the whole town, and yet the words still hurt just as badly. But then again, that was when she thought he'd pulled the sick prank.

She *still* thought he had. She'd pulled herself up on the corner of the desk he had brought in for her a few days earlier, her legs dangling and crossed at the ankles. She'd leaned her hands back on the cold metal and was eyeing him speculatively, her expression doubtful.

"You act as if you're surprised that it is *your* brand on *your* cattle," she said, narrowing her gaze on him. "Why is that?"

He shrugged defensively. "Because while I freely admit they are my cattle, I have no idea how they got here."

"Ri-i-ght," she said, drawing out the word. "I'm sure they just wandered in here on their own. Maybe they were hanging around last evening after a night on the town and decided they'd visit my spa and get their hair done. Did you give them the key?"

"Snarky much?"

"Well, excuse me for being a little skeptical. It seems to me that all the pieces fit together to make a pretty clear picture of what happened. The evidence against you seems airtight."

"Yeah," he agreed, "except for one thing."

"And that is?"

"Me. I'd hoped you knew me better than to assume I could do anything so—"

"Stupid?"

He glared at her. "I was going to say dishonorable, but stupid works, too."

Her gaze turned from challenging to hesitant and he pressed his advantage, hoping he could convince her of his innocence, although at this point he wasn't sure if it mattered.

"Some other knucklehead put these heifers in here. Not me."

"But who? And why?"

He frowned. "That's what we've got to figure out. First, though, I'm going to clean up this mess."

She laid a hand on his arm. "*We* will clean up this mess. It's my salon, after all."

Even though Nick wasn't the one who'd pulled off the thoughtless prank, he still felt guilty about it, though he couldn't fathom why. Maybe because they were his heifers. Or maybe it was something else—something nagging at the back of his mind that he couldn't yet put his finger on. But he thought it might have something to do with the wounded look in Vivian's eyes when she'd accused him of making fun of her.

He herded the cattle out the back door and corralled them with some old crates, then retrieved the shovel and broom from the bed of his truck. He and Viv worked in uncomfortable silence, Nick shoveling and Vivian sweeping.

He imagined she was thinking the same thing he was—who was responsible for this juvenile prank? Local teenagers out on a lark? Someone with a grudge against Vivian?

He couldn't imagine the latter. Vivian might not be everyone's cup of tea but she was one of the sweetest women he'd ever met. She'd give a stranger one of her kidneys if they asked her for it. That was just the kind of person she was. Full of heart and genuine compassion.

No, it couldn't have anything to do with a personal grudge against her, or the salon. So what was it, then?

Dusk had fallen by the time they were finished. He scooped the cow patties into a pile near the back door and then transferred them into the field that bordered behind. The stench inside the building wouldn't go away anytime soon but at least Viv wouldn't be stepping on cow patties every time she turned around.

"I'll bring a trailer over here to pick up the stock," he told her, leaning against the shovel and wiping the sweat off his brow with the corner of his shirt. "And then we'll do a little bit of detective work, figure out who did this to you, and why. And how they managed to use my cattle to pull off the prank. I really apologize, Vivian."

"What? Why? You didn't do anything. I should be the one apologizing to you. I jumped all over you. I feel really bad that I blamed you without proof."

"As if the open door and my brand on the cattle weren't enough proof. Thank you for believing me, though."

She smiled at him and his stomach flipped over. He must be overtired from all the work he'd been doing. Or hungry. He refused to consider that what he was feeling could be any more than that.

"Did you want to ride with me back to my ranch?" he asked. "I can drop you by your place afterward. That way you won't have to worry about the stench of cattle following you into your car."

She glanced down at her now-dirty sneakers and frowned. "Would you mind? Alexis can drive me back here later to pick up my car."

"Not at all. It'll only take a few minutes to hitch up the trailer and I could use the company."

They talked on the way over to the Circle M, but not about the cattle or the prank. He needed time to mull what had happened over in his head and he imagined Viv felt the same. Instead, Viv chatted steadily about the floral wallpaper she was considering and the specialty massage chairs where a woman could apparently get her feet soaked and her toenails painted while the chair worked on the sore muscles in her back and neck.

That was what a spa was all about? It kind of sounded awesome.

The barbershop certainly didn't offer amenities comparable to that.

Not that he wanted his toenails painted. But a massage now and again would be nice.

They reached his ranch and he backed his truck up to his smallest trailer.

"Just hang out here for a moment while I hook 'er up," he said. "It won't take me long."

"In the dark? How can you see what you're doing?" She sounded impressed. His ego ballooned slightly, which felt good, after having it bashed so badly earlier in the day.

He chuckled. "I've had years of practice."

He hopped out of the cab and had just reached the hitch when he heard loud chortling coming from inside the barn. He turned toward the noise, frowning.

He knew that sound. He'd heard it a thousand times growing up—his youngest brother, Slade, trying to pull one over on him, get him in trouble for something he hadn't done. Slade had been forever trying to dupe him or frame him, although Nick had gotten him back far more often than Slade had been able to prank him.

Prank *him*.

Unbelievable. This had never been about Vivian at all.

He growled and strode into the barn. He was going to knock Slade's head so hard he'd see stars.

"What were you thinking?" he demanded into the darkness, even before he could see the outline of his brother. "Do you have any idea what you've done?"

Slade burst forward, laughing and slapping Nick on the back.

"Good one, huh?" he asked. "I would have loved to see your face when you walked into that shop and saw your cattle hanging out there, big brother."

Nick grabbed the collar of Slade's shirt and gave him a shake. "It wasn't me who found the heifers, you blooming idiot. It was Vivian, and she was alone. Let's just say she was not pleased."

"Uh-oh," Slade said. "I figured you guys would be together when you discovered the stock at the shop. I didn't scare her, did I?"

"Probably. A little. Mostly you made her

angry—not to mention making an absolute mess of the building. How did you get in, anyway?"

Slade grinned. "I still remember how to pick a lock. And I've got to say, that one wasn't very solid. Vivian ought to look into something a little sturdier."

"I'll let her know you think so," Nick replied, allowing sarcasm to creep into his voice. "Now, let's go. Viv is waiting in the truck and you owe her an apology."

"It was only a joke," Slade muttered, sounding just the same as he had when he'd been caught with his hand in the cookie jar as a child. Apparently getting married and becoming a father hadn't brought Slade to full maturity. Probably nothing ever would. He might be a policeman now, but goofing around was just Slade's nature. That didn't absolve him from the error of his ways, though.

"If it was a joke, it was a tasteless one," Nick felt obligated to point out. "How long have you and Laney been married now, and yet it never occurred to you that it might hurt a woman's feelings to put livestock in the shop she's working so hard to remodel?"

At least Slade had the good grace to wince and look apologetic at Nick's words.

Nick grabbed him by the elbow and half pushed, half dragged him back to the truck. He opened the passenger side door and leaned against the door frame.

"I have a dolt of a brother here who has something to say to you."

Not surprisingly, Vivian's gaze widened in surprise, especially when she saw who he was with.

"Slade? What's going on here?"

"What's going on," Nick replied before Slade could get a word in edgewise, "is that this idiot thought it would be funny to play a prank on *me* by putting my own cattle in the shop where I was working."

"A prank on *you*?" Vivian parroted, clearly stunned. "You mean this wasn't about me at all?"

"I didn't mean any harm by it," Slade said. "I thought it would be funny."

He would. Nick grunted in frustration. How was he supposed to explain the intricacies of the relationship between brothers, the masculine give-and-take? It probably wouldn't make a bit of sense to a woman, especially one as delicate as Vivian.

"It wasn't funny," Nick growled. "You hurt her feelings. Do you have any idea how she felt when she realized someone had broken into her shop and had left live cattle there?"

"They made quite a mess," Vivian admitted. "And they smell, by the way." She dropped her head into her hands and her shoulders quivered.

Nick had never felt so uncomfortable in his life. He wanted to shake Slade until his teeth rattled. Slade had been the instigator, but at the end of the day, Nick felt that he was the one responsible for making Vivian cry. He might not have been the perpetrator of the prank, but it wouldn't have happened if he hadn't been working with her.

"We're both really sorry," Nick said, and Vivian made a choking sound. "Viv? Are you all right?"

She looked up then, and there were indeed tears in her eyes, but it wasn't because she was crying. She was laughing so hard her cheeks had turned a bright pink and her breath was coming in quick, uneven hiccups.

"Doesn't your wife know that she should keep you on a leash?" she teased, shaking her finger at Slade and giving his shoulder a friendly shove.

Slade flashed his lady-killer grin. "I'm afraid I have the tendency to escape from time to time."

"And just look at what happens," Nick said.

"It's only a little mischief," Vivian insisted. "No harm done."

No harm done? After everything Vivian had been through tonight, she was being extremely gracious. They'd had to spend hours cleaning up the mess. And the lingering smell wouldn't do her any favors. Weren't pregnant women supposed to be especially sensitive to strong smells?

For all of that, he wasn't quite as ready to let his rascally brother off the hook.

"You owe her," he insisted. "We've already cleaned up after the cattle, but it still smells like livestock and probably will for quite some time. The least you can do is put some man hours in. We've got some walls and floors that need scrubbing and then new drywall needs to be put in."

To his credit, Slade grinned and nodded. "Sure, I'd be happy to help. Say the word and I'll be there. Just tell me when. And again, Vivian, I'm really sorry. I didn't mean anything by it. It was a stupid thing to do and I'm an idiot."

"Think nothing of it," she insisted. "I've forgotten it already."

Nick knew that wasn't the case. She'd be remembering the prank every time she walked into her shop and inhaled the after-effects of livestock for a long time to come.

"I'm really sorry," Nick apologized once again when they were in the truck and headed toward Viv's cabin. "I can't believe my brother would pull such a lame prank. I thought he was smarter than that. But he's always had a habit of not thinking things all the way through."

"The truth is, I like Slade, and I'm sure Jax is a stand-up guy as well, but I wouldn't be surprised if you're the smartest of the three McKenna brothers," Vivian suggested, a smile tugging at her lips.

"Oh, there's no question about that."

A giggle escaped her. "And modest, too. I picked a real winner at the auction, didn't I?"

"If you don't count the cattle with my brand on them ending up inside your shop."

"I don't hold it against you," she assured him. "I'm not even upset with your brother, although I do wonder where his head was at—and where his wife was when he pulled the caper off. Can you imagine him trying to sneak a couple of cows into a shop on Main Street? I guess it's a good thing he's a cop, or he might have gotten arrested."

"Maybe some time behind bars would do him good," Nick growled. "Get him to think a little bit."

"It's okay, Nick. Really."

"You have a bigger heart than I do. I'm not sure I can let this go so easily."

"As pranks go, it may have been way out there, but at the end of the day, there's no real harm done. I believe in the Golden Rule—do to others whatever you would have them do to you. I actually benefited from it in a way, because now Slade feels honor-bound to put some man hours into my salon. Call me crazy, but I'm actually relieved."

"Relieved? How are you relieved? Because the prank wasn't aimed at you?"

"No. Because you weren't the one responsible. For a moment there I thought maybe you really disliked me, or at least that you didn't want me opening the spa. I want to make sure you're sticking around this time because you see the potential in what I'm doing and not because of some misplaced sense of obligation. You've more than fulfilled any obligation from that stupid auction. You know that, right?"

He glanced over at her. She was such a striking woman, with her golden hair silhouetted against the moonlight in the dark cab, that his breath snagged in his throat. He wasn't certain he was staying for *all* the right reasons, definitely not for the genuine motives Vivian was suggesting.

No—he was starting to think he was sticking around for the *wrong* reasons. He was feeling all muddled up inside his head. Confused. Part of him felt like bolting. And yet he couldn't even consider walking away from this project—or walking away from Vivian.

"Does that mean you're going to let me stick around?" he asked, his voice deep and husky. He held his breath as he waited for the answer, then released it in a slow sigh of relief when she agreed. He still wasn't up to analyzing his feelings, but he knew for certain that right or wrong, he wanted to stay in Viv's life.

Chapter Five

❧

Anticipating a large crowd for whatever sports television-viewing party that was currently all the rage at Cup O' Jo's, Vivian arrived early and secured her spot—*their* spots. Hers and Nick's. She'd selected a booth near the biggest large-screen TV for Nick's sake. She certainly had no interest in whatever game had everyone in town so excited.

This was the first and most likely the only time she would *ever* gather with others in town to watch—baseball, was it? She loved a party as much as the next social butterfly, but anything to do with sports...

Not her kettle of tea, by any means. At all.

But Nick had been so adamant about wanting to make it up to her for the silly stunt his brother had pulled that he'd practically begged her to come to the game with him.

She couldn't imagine why he continued to feel guilty over the cattle incident. She had assured him repeatedly that she'd put the whole thing behind her and held no ill will toward Slade—and especially not toward Nick, who had done nothing but help her. As far as she was concerned, he was at least as much a victim in the prank as she had been. Slade had been aiming his mischief at Nick, not Vivian.

Still, Nick kept insisting on making reparation, and for some inexplicable reason, he thought hanging out together to watch a sports game of some sort qualified as making things right. He'd said something about how he knew she loved a good party.

She didn't have the heart to tell him she wouldn't know a football from that thingamajig the hockey guys hit around the ice with their sticks. She would be bored stiff and had no inclination whatsoever to even try to figure out the rules of the game. But if it meant that much to Nick for her to be there with him, she decided it wouldn't hurt her to put aside a couple of hours of her time and be a good *sport* about it.

She snorted aloud at her own unintended pun and then clapped a palm over her mouth, not wanting to be seen as the crazy lady in the corner laughing to herself.

Fortunately for her own reputation for sanity, Nick appeared in the doorway and Vivian waved him over. His eyes lit up and his grin sent a kaleidoscope of butterflies loose in her stomach.

"What's so funny?" he asked as he approached.

"Funny?"

Rats. She'd been discovered laughing at herself, and by Nick, no less.

"I, errr... N-nothing," she stammered.

He reached for the chair across the table from her and then paused. She thought it might be because he'd realized she was facing the big-screen television and he would be able to see better if he sat next to her and not across from her—not that she'd *intentionally* planned for that to happen.

Her cheeks warmed under his scrutiny.

"Is there a problem?" she asked when he didn't take his seat, either next to her *or* across from her.

"What in the world are you wearing?" he blurted out, staring at her as if she were an exotic animal at the local zoo.

Her face went from warm to burning hot

and her nerves tingled with affront. Was he seriously dissing her on her fashion choices?

She'd spent extra time dressing today. She glanced down at her outfit but saw nothing amiss in what she'd chosen. A cute sports jersey—the only one she had—dark-wash blue jeans and decorative cowboy boots.

But Nick's tone wasn't complimentary in the least. He sounded horrified, and she felt terribly self-conscious. She rose one brow and tipped up her chin at him.

"A Denver Broncos jersey," he mumbled, answering his own question. He pinched his lips tightly and she thought for a moment he was angry, but then he sputtered and his blue eyes glimmered with amusement.

She still didn't see the problem, nor why he was so entertained by her choice in clothing. She would have him know *she* was one of the few women who was blessed to be able to actually *rock* the color orange.

"I guess so," she answered reluctantly. "My cousin who lives in Colorado gave it to me last Christmas. It's the only sports clothing I own so I thought it would be appropriate for the occasion."

He laughed and dropped into the seat beside her, his arm around the back of the booth, just short of resting across her shoulders.

"Honey, I hate to be the one to break it to you, but Serendipity is located plumb in the middle of Texas. It's probably not the best idea for you to be wandering around with another state's team jersey on. You probably don't realize it, but you run the risk of being mobbed by rabid fans." A chuckle escaped him but he made a vain attempt to bite it back.

"Oh," she said, defeated at the notion that she'd somehow erred in her fashion choices. She had a reputation to maintain, after all, to look put-together at all times. She planned on opening a beauty salon and spa. She couldn't go around looking like she didn't know how to dress herself. "That bad, huh?"

He winced. "And there's more."

"More?" She was appalled by the prospect. What had she done now?

He cleared his throat before speaking. "You, uh, have the wrong sport. You're wearing a football jersey. We're here to watch a baseball game."

"Does it matter?"

His gaze widened, and he started to nod but then stopped short.

"You know what? No. No it doesn't." His lips twitched at one corner. "At least, not to me, it doesn't. There are more...*intense* fans who might take issue with your apparel."

Viv couldn't imagine why it should matter so much. It was just for a stupid sports game, and it was only a shirt, after all. The point ought to be that she'd taken extra attention with her appearance today.

For the party. Not for Nick's sake. But if it was going to bother him...

"Should I go home and change?"

"You're not going anywhere. If someone has a problem with your jersey they'll have to go through me."

At first his statement ruffled her feathers, sounding as imperious as it did, but there was something about the thought of him looking out for her best interests that smoothed her emotional feathers back into place. He was only offering to protect her from her own fashion mistake, after all. There was some chivalry to that.

"We should probably order now before the crowd gets any bigger," she suggested. "Did you want to get an appetizer, or maybe dessert?"

He grinned and pulled her deeper into the

crook of his shoulder. "Both. And whatever Chance is cooking up for the special of the day in between the two. I think I heard something about roast beef and gravy over a mound of mashed potatoes. Or if you don't want that, you can choose something different. This day is all about you, remember?"

Vivian really wasn't that hungry. It didn't help that her stomach was fluttering. She'd thought her morning sickness was finally getting better, but it appeared to be returning today in diamonds.

Jo approached their table with her pad in one hand and a pencil in the other, wearing a T-shirt that read "Here we go, Let's go, Here we go (Clap! Clap!)"

Viv couldn't help but think that was a pretty good approximation of the way she was feeling. She ordered a Caesar salad and a ginger ale just to mollify Nick. Hopefully the carbonation would settle her stomach.

He looked as if he were about to protest how little she was getting but then shook his head and turned his attention toward the café's vivacious owner. "We'll have the flowering onion appetizer with every kind of dipping sauce you've got. Give us a family-style helping of your special of the day.

I think we'll wait until the seventh-inning stretch to order dessert, but be sure to swing by our table then."

"Swing by your table." Jo cackled and slapped him on the shoulder. "Good one, Nick."

She bustled off with their order and Nick turned to face Vivian. "A salad? Really? I'm treating you to dinner and all you order is a salad?"

Vivian shrugged dismissively. A salad was her standard order, and she didn't see why she should change it just because she was here with Nick, or because he was paying for it.

"I'm trying to make up for all the trouble my brother caused you," he reminded her. "You're not making this easy on me."

So…what? She was supposed to stuff herself with unnecessary carbs to make him feel better? She didn't need to be reminded that he was the only reason why she was sitting here in the wrong-colored sports jersey waiting for a baseball game to start in which she had no interest.

"I'll order a warm brownie sundae for dessert," she said, deciding that giving in to him would be easier than trying to explain her

way out of it. Bye-bye, watching her diet for
the baby's sake. But she couldn't see bickering over her choice of a salad. And Baby
G did seem to have a preference for sweets
lately. She'd been craving chocolate like
crazy.

And jalapeños, but she thought Nick might
not like having her add them as a side to
their dessert.

She sat stiffly, watching excited townspeople funneling into the café, the volume
in the room increasing exponentially with
every new arrival. The folks in Serendipity loved a good party and they took their
sports seriously.

Vivian generally enjoyed social gather-
ings. In any other situation she'd be fluttering
from table to table, talking to all her friends
and neighbors. But after what Nick had said,
she was ultra-aware of her clothing—bright
orange in a sea of white. She didn't care for
the possibility of offending anyone, however unintentionally, so she stayed where
she was—tucked under Nick's arm.

She was surprised to see Alexis and Griff
enter the café. Her twin was no more of a
sports lover than she was, or at least she
hadn't been before. Vivian felt a sudden gap

in her heart. She'd been away from home for far too long. Even though Serendipity was as slow moving as a rock, much had changed in the years she'd been gone.

She waved to catch Alexis's attention. Alexis smiled as she grabbed Griff's hand and guided him over to Viv and Nick's table.

"Are these seats taken?" Alexis asked, gesturing to the empty side of the booth. Alexis's curious gaze swept over both of them and she smirked, raising her eyebrows in an unspoken query. As twins, Viv and Alexis had always been able to communicate without speaking.

Vivian didn't like what Alexis was saying.

Appalled, she shook her head vigorously. She'd been so busy worrying about her fashion faux pas that she hadn't even considered the unspoken message she was sending to anyone who bothered looking. She was sitting far too close to Nick, and his arm's position was a little bit too possessive. If Alexis was getting the wrong impression, she could only imagine what the rest of her friends and neighbors were thinking. The last thing she needed right now was to be fodder for the gossip mill.

She didn't have to worry for long. Once

the game began, everyone's attentions were glued to the screen. A few minutes later Jo arrived with the enormous appetizer. It was more than enough for everyone at the table and Nick invited Alexis and Griff to share.

Viv caught her sister's eye.

"Powder our noses?" she asked, just as the crowd roared in excitement over whatever boring thing was happening on the big screen.

Alexis agreed and they picked their way through the crowd to the relative quiet of the restroom. Alexis immediately grabbed Viv's elbow and twisted her around.

"You've been keeping secrets from me, girl," she accused good-naturedly. "Spill it."

"I don't have any secrets. There's nothing to spill," she assured her twin, but her voice sounded high and strained even to her own ears.

"Oh, so that's why you're sitting so close to Nick McKenna—and why he had his arm around you? Because there is nothing going on I ought to know about?"

"I wasn't—he didn't—" Vivian started to protest, but then sputtered to a stop.

"Since when are you two an item?" Alexis continued, laughing. "I seem to have missed the memo, and I'm your sister. How fair is that?"

Viv looked away and turned on the tap, splashing cold water on her face to counter the blush she knew had risen to her cheeks.

"It's a business arrangement," she assured Alexis, although one glance at her sister's reflection told her that her twin wasn't buying it for a second. "I won him in the auction, remember?"

"Which still doesn't explain why you are at Cup O' Jo's for a meal and a game. That doesn't sound like a work obligation. Actually, it sounds a lot more like a *date* to me."

"Well, it isn't." Viv yanked a couple of paper towels from the dispenser and dabbed at the water droplets on her chin. "It's a long story. His brother Slade played a prank on me the other day. For some reason, Nick felt responsible for it. He wanted to make it up to me by taking me to a party, and here we are."

"Okay. If you say so."

"And don't ask me about why we're watching a sports game, because I do not know the answer to that question."

Alexis tittered. "I wouldn't think of it."

Vivian sighed dramatically. "Moving on?"

Alexis shrugged, letting her off the hook

for now, but Viv knew she hadn't heard the last of it. Her twin sister was too perceptive by far, compounded by the fact that they were identical twins who practically lived in each other's minds.

She was toast and she knew it.

"So... A business arrangement, then," Alexis prodded. "How's the remodeling going, by the way? I hardly ever see you anymore."

Vivian let out a breath, happy for the temporary reprieve and change in subject.

"Slower than I'd like. We had to gut the whole shop and start rebuilding from the ground up. Nick has been a great help to me there," she admitted grudgingly.

"Ironic, isn't it?"

"What's that?"

"That of all the men in town, grizzly ol' Nick is the one you chose to help you build your pastel, feminine spa. Talk about the opposite end of the spectrum from what your future clientele will look like."

"I should hope so. Anyway, he's good with a hammer. I can worry about finding customers later—a construction guy is what I need right now."

Alexis nodded. "So I've heard. Do you

ever wonder, though, what he might look like all cleaned up? Shave and a haircut, two bits?"

"No," Viv replied without skipping a beat.

"You have to admit he's handsome, even with all that scruff."

Vivian didn't want to talk about this. She didn't even want to *think* about it.

"Imagine what you could do with a guy like that. Make him into a new man." Alexis's blue eyes glittered in the soft fluorescent lighting.

"No," Vivian said again. She didn't need a GPS to see where this was going.

"You should do it."

Viv's shoulders tightened with strain. The signs were clear. *Dangerous Curves Ahead.* "Do what?"

She didn't really want to know.

She already knew.

"Make him over."

"Yeah. So not happening. Do you think he's going to let me anywhere near him with a sharp pair of shears and a straight razor?"

"You're a clever woman. I'm sure you can figure something out."

"No."

"Come on. I dare you. Make Nick over by

the end of the day of your Grand Openings and I'll do your laundry for a month. If you lose, you can do mine."

Viv *had* been bringing her wash over to Alexis's house once a week since she'd moved back to Serendipity. Her little cabin didn't come with laundry facilities. It sure would save her time if she could have Alexis do the hauling—plus the sorting and folding.

"Three months," she countered.

"Two," Alexis responded cheerfully. "Deal?"

Vivian wondered why she'd allowed Alexis to talk her into this. She sighed.

"All right, already," she reluctantly conceded, knowing Alexis wasn't going to let it go. "You win. I'll do it. But don't forget. My laundry. Two months."

Back in the shop, Nick spent the next week cleaning out all the debris left in the back of the building and framing what would eventually become Viv's office. He was exhausted almost to his breaking point, between working on Viv's renovation, doing all his ranch work and occasionally helping with the construction of the senior center, but he kept on pushing through it. He felt as if he were being drawn and quartered, being pulled in so many different directions, but it was all important. Every last bit of it.

He was determined to make the renovation area in the future salon safe for Vivian—and most especially for her baby. Viv had blatantly refused his *suggestion* that she stay at home and take care of herself and her little one until all of the construction work was completed. She absolutely nixed the idea of supervising from a distance. Whatever else the woman was, she was hands-on where her business was concerned. She wasn't afraid to get dirty, and she had such a fantastic attitude about it all—always looking for some way to make every task fun. She was enthusiastic and fully committed in everything she did.

She'd be a great mom.

But what made her a good businesswoman and a great mother was exactly the trait that was going to drive him crazy before he could get this remodel finished.

Vivian was currently located in what would be the office when he was done putting up the drywall. She was hunched over the dingy metal desk, straining to see under the dim light of a gooseneck lamp.

She was working with some spreadsheets she'd printed with her prehistoric printer. Her mouth was, thankfully, covered with the dust mask he'd convinced her to wear. There was that, at least. She'd listened to him about precisely one thing.

A small victory, to be sure, but a victory nonetheless. He'd take what he could where Viv was concerned.

He turned back to his work, measuring and cutting two-by-fours on a table saw. The saw was shooting up clouds of sawdust and he didn't want her breathing it in.

He could be just as stubborn as she was. He hoped. He absolutely refused to have her underfoot in the open construction area, where another mishap like the one that had happened a few weeks ago could occur.

Why hadn't Vivian mentioned she was pregnant when she'd first won him at auction? If he was going to be her general contractor, that seemed to him like an awfully large piece of information to exclude. Her safety was in his hands, as events had proven.

Had she been *trying* to hide her condition? And if so...why?

The secret, if that's what it had been, was out now, and Vivian didn't seem to be mind-ing the extra attention and support she was receiving from her friends—including him.

But that didn't stop him from feeling like an idiot now that he knew the truth. *How* had he not known? He couldn't believe he'd been so completely unobservant. Now that he knew what he was looking for, it was impossible for him not to see—the fluttery, over-size shirts, the rosy pink in her cheeks, the sparkle in her blue eyes.

Yep. She was pregnant, all right.

He was an idiot.

And now he felt more responsible than ever for making sure the renovation went off without a hitch. He still had his doubts about the probability of success for her business in Serendipity, but he would do everything he could to help it prosper, if only because he now knew she was going to be a single mom. She'd told him definitively that the father was not in the picture, so she needed to be able to make a living to support herself and her child.

He cast her a sideways glance, noting the way some of her blond hair had escaped a loose bun and was now framing her face like sunshine around a cloud. Usually her face was full of sunshine, too…but not right now.

He worried about her stress level. He couldn't see much of her face around the breathing mask she was wearing, but he noticed the worry lines across her forehead, and her body language was speaking volumes.

Her eyes were narrowed on the spreadsheets in front of her and she was mercilessly tapping the pencil she was holding. Her drooping shoulders suggested she wasn't getting as much sleep as she ought to be.

He set the wood he was working with aside, brushed the sawdust from his jeans and moved to the door frame.

"You okay?"

She dropped her pencil and looked up in surprise, her eyes wide, as if he'd startled her. Apparently she hadn't been aware of him, or the sudden silence after the persistent sound of the saw biting into the wood.

"If your eyes were laser beams that pile of papers would be ashes by now."

She pulled her mask down and smiled, but her face was creased with tired lines. She looked as wiped out as he felt. That couldn't be good for the baby.

"You've been staring at those numbers for two hours at least. Don't you think you ought to take a little break and walk around a bit?

Stretch your legs? Your ledgers aren't going anywhere."

She sighed and stretched, pressing the small of her back. "You're right. I lost track of time. There's just so much to organize. I'm afraid I'm not going to be able to get it all together by the date of my grand opening."

Nick was also afraid, although he didn't share his fears with Viv. It was very clear that she hadn't realized how extensive the renovations would need to be when she'd bought the building. Whatever plans she made, he doubted she'd allocated enough time or money for this stage. Was she feeling the pinch now?

Her brother-in-law, Griff, had helped her start her business in Houston and Nick knew he was assisting her with her current business plan as well, but the responsibilities still had to weigh heavily on her shoulders. Even though Nick's first impression of Viv was that she was a bubblehead, he'd revised his opinion of her since then. She came off as warm and effervescent and possibly a little ditzy in personality, but inside her heart beat a proud woman determined to make her spa succeed on her own merit. She allowed nothing to go unnoticed and was personally involved in every single area of the remodel.

He believed that *she* thought she had the strength to do it on her own. Still, he couldn't help but think she might be over her head.

Add to that the fact that she would soon be caring for an infant and was even now dealing with the unique trials of being pregnant. Aching back. Tired feet. Morning sickness.

She needed his help. That was all there was to it. And whether she wanted him or not, he was going to be there until the end.

He was way past wondering how he'd gotten into this mess. His big worry now was how he would ever get out of it. Vivian's problems—and by extension his own—were only just beginning. They had a long path ahead of them.

"Put that all aside for now and go enjoy a walk," he suggested to her.

"Only if you'll agree to walk with me," she said, picking up the soft pink sweater she'd hung over the back of the chair.

He stepped up and took the sweater from her hands and then helped her slip into it. He slid his palms across her shoulders to smooth the soft material and felt her muscles tighten under his fingers.

With effort, he resisted the instinctive impulse to knead the stress from her muscles, knowing she might take it the wrong way. With the sweet floral scent of her perfume wafting over his senses and making his head spin with her nearness, he was having difficulty remaining impartial himself.

"There you are, then." He cleared his throat and stepped back, reminding himself why all this was necessary.

Her baby.

"Thank you." She flashed a grateful smile at him from over her shoulder, her cheeks the same pretty shade of pink as her sweater, and his throat tightened around his breath.

Not helping.

"Er—my pleasure." The words were an automatic response, but to his astonishment, he realized he really meant them.

Really not helping.

Fighting the urge to flee the scene entirely, he opened the door for her and gestured both directions along the clapboard sidewalk. Part of Serendipity's charm was that the buildings on Main Street still retained an old-fashioned Western flavor to their storefronts. Cup O' Jo's Café even sported a hitching post and water trough out front. Emerson's Hardware had three wooden rocking chairs under its eave, almost always occupied by three old fellows in matching bib overalls.

"Any particular destination?" he asked.

"No, not really," she replied, her voice sounding as if her thoughts were distant.

Nick examined the sidewalk each way and then turned left, determining that the clapboard that direction was in better condition. Besides, if they walked that direction they'd pass the park, where they would be able to stroll along the well-paved bike path—in full view of the community.

Couldn't hurt. He needed to remember what he was potentially getting out of this... *business* arrangement. The opportunity to redeem himself. Although thinking in those terms might actually be sabotaging his goal.

Was it selfish to want to use this to prove himself trustworthy with a woman? With Vivian?

They didn't speak as they crossed the street at the one and only stoplight in town and meandered down to the park. He tucked her arm through his elbow to offer her extra support.

He sensed something was bothering her beyond the obvious, but he hesitated to ask what it was. What good would that do him, other than drag him deeper into the quandary of the mind that was Vivian Grainger?

Anyway, if she thought he could help with whatever was keeping her thoughts so occupied, she'd ask him, right?

After a few minutes he gestured to a park bench. As soon as she sat down, she turned toward him. Worry shadowed her eyes but she smiled nonetheless.

"It's a glorious day, isn't it?" she asked, flicking her hair over her shoulder with one hand. "I'm glad you suggested the walk."

Glorious day? Who even talked like that?

Vivian, apparently. Even when she was distracted by her problems.

"Yeah," he agreed. "It's nice."

He nodded his head in acknowledgment to a couple of female joggers, whom he recognized were old friends of Brittany's. They seemed stunned to see him sitting companionably with Vivian. He smiled at their expressions.

See? he wanted to tell them. *Not every woman in town thinks I'm a leper.*

"Well, that was rude," Vivian observed with a wry grin, her voice dripping as sour as lemon juice.

He switched his gaze from Brittany's

friends to Vivian, wondering what he'd missed. He hadn't seen either of the ladies do or say something untoward. If they had, he would catch up to them and call them out on it. No one was going to be discourteous to Viv on his watch.

He hated to reveal his ignorance, but he had to ask. "What did they do?"

"What did *they* do?" Vivian's gaze widened on him and she pursed her lips. "What did *they* do? Take a good look in the mirror, buddy. Didn't your mama teach you that it's not polite to check out other women when you are currently in the company of one?"

"What? No, I—"

She arched an eyebrow.

"Vivian, honestly." He raised both hands in a gesture of truthfulness and surrender. "You've got to believe me. I promise I wasn't checking out those women, or at least not in the way you're thinking."

"No? It certainly looked that way to me. I saw where your gaze went. Not that I blame you. Brooke and Ashley are lovely women. I'm sure either one of them would be thrilled if you asked them out on a date."

He cringed. If only she knew just how wrong she was. On all counts. He wouldn't be interested in asking either one of them for a date, and they definitely wouldn't agree to go out with him if he did ask.

"Yeah, that's kind of the point." He blew out a breath, feeling his face warm under her scrutiny. "Actually, I was kind of hoping they'd notice me. Er—well, not notice *me*, so much as observe that I was sitting here with you."

"With *me*?" she exclaimed. "Okay, buster, now you've lost me completely."

"I know you may find this hard to believe, but I don't have a stellar reputation with the ladies around here," he reluctantly explained, then cringed at how egotistical he sounded. "The truth of it is, I doubt whether either one of those women would go on a date with me if I asked. Not that I want to ask," he quickly amended.

"I *do* find that hard to believe." Her gaze warmed as she looked him over. His stomach flipped. Those blue eyes were downright dangerous when they were directed at him. "I can't imagine any young lady not giving you a chance."

What was she saying? That she found him attractive? He remembered back to the day of the auction when he'd thought that dating might have been on her mind, that it might have been the reason she bid on him.

And how laughable was that? It was no wonder Brittany had felt it necessary to burst his bubble in public. His ego was so huge it could rival one of those balloons at the Macy's Thanksgiving Day Parade.

Vivian's life was full—more than full—between her coming baby and her fledgling business. She wouldn't have time for a relationship even if she wanted one, which he highly doubted. She hadn't ever mentioned the baby's father, but he didn't appear to be part of Viv's life.

He wouldn't burden her further. Instead, he turned the conversation back to himself.

"You know Brittany Evans, right?"

"Sure. Not well, though. She was two grades above me in school, as I recall. Pretty brunette. She was a cheerleader and tended to only associate with those in her...'social sphere.'"

Nick snorted. "That's a kind way of saying she was one of the leaders of a clique of snobby popular girls."

"Was she? I guess I never noticed."

No, Viv wouldn't have. Even as a teenager, she was the kind of person who was friends with everyone, from the loftiest cheerleader, the star quarterback, and the drum major of the marching band all the way to every kid in the special education classes.

Brittany, on the other hand…

What had he been thinking, dating her? She was physically attractive, but her personality had always grated on him. Why was he only now seeing how miserable their whole relationship had been?

He'd been poor boyfriend material because his heart hadn't really been in it. Brittany had had every right to trash-talk him.

"We were dating for a while," he explained ruefully. "Let's just say I didn't pay as much attention to her as she deserved, and she let me know it."

"I see." Viv paused and then shook her head. "Well, no, actually, I guess I don't see. What does all that have to do with me?"

Her words sounded suspicious and she narrowed her gaze on him.

"We had a big, very *public* breakup last New Year's Eve at the community party. Brittany basically lambasted me in front of the whole town for being an unfeeling jerk. She called me all kinds of names. She warned the single women in Serendipity—in a very loud voice—that they ought to beware." A self-deprecating laugh escaped through his pinched lips. "That was pretty much the end of my social life as I once knew it."

It was only now, as he related the story to Vivian, that he comprehended how little it mattered to him. Over the past year of forced solitude, he'd realized he was okay being alone, with just himself for company. Perhaps he was a perennial bachelor after all and not, as he'd always believed himself to be, a man who would eventually settle down with a wife and family.

Maybe he'd never had that in him at all.

"So let me get this straight," Viv said, interrupting his thoughts. "You wanted Ashley and Brooke—who are friends of Brittany's, if I'm remembering right—to notice we're together so they would get the mistaken impression that you're *dating* me? That you've moved on?"

Her eyes widened and she sniffed in astonishment. "That was what the whole point of dinner at Cup O' Jo's was about, wasn't it? To let the town know you've moved on—with me. I feel like I've suddenly been caught up in a high school drama. Grow up, Nick."

Her words hit him like a brick to the chest.

Maybe it was because she was speaking the truth.

"That's what I'm trying to do."

His first instinct was to defend himself and his actions, but instead he put all of his effort into tamping down the flare of his ego. He blew out a breath, took off his hat and scrubbed his fingers through his hair. "I know it looks and sounds bad, and I get that you're angry with me, but this was never about giving anyone the mistaken impression that we're a couple."

"No? Then what?" Her voice and expression softened. He couldn't blame her for jumping to a negative conclusion, like she had with the cattle in her shop, but this time—just like last time—she seemed willing to hear him out when he tried to explain.

"I'm trying to prove to the town—and to myself—that I'm not a total muck-up. That's what Brittany said—that no one should ever rely on me because I'd always let them down. I thought maybe if I could help you get your shop fixed up, it would show that I really can be relied on. That you were right to trust me to do the remodeling job for you. I hoped maybe you could even be my friend. But I've kind of blown it now, haven't I?"

"Yes, you have," Vivian replied with a grave frown. Then her nose started twitching and a moment later she was giggling. "Oh, Nick, you take yourself—and life in general—way too seriously. You need to loosen up."

He lowered his brow and replaced his cowboy hat. Was she making fun of him?

"I'm a typical firstborn," he snapped back. "What do you expect?"

"I know what *you* expect out of yourself. Perfection. Which none of us can really aspire to, can we? All I'm saying is you shouldn't be so hard on yourself all the time."

He raised his brow, questioning her statement. She was one to talk. He'd heard her speak negatively of herself more times than he could count.

She shook her head. They weren't going to talk about her. They never did.

"You know Serendipity," she continued, not allowing him to redirect their conversation. "Yes, folks love to gossip. And your breakup with Brittany probably was big news—until about January 2nd, when some new item of interest popped up to gain the gossips' attention. After that you and Brittany were yesterday's news and everyone moved on from there to new ground. You're probably the only one who remembers it."

"Do you think?" The relief flooding through him was palpable, sluicing over his muscles and loosening his joints and marrow until his whole body felt lighter, almost as if he were floating. He hadn't realized what a heavy weight he'd been carrying. And Vivian, with her sweet, kind words, had set him free.

"Oh, I'm sure of it. And if I'm not mistaken, Brittany has put it in the past, as well. I heard just the other day that she's engaged to Gregory Carr. Apparently it didn't take her too long to get over you, so I wouldn't beat yourself up about it."

Vivian was right. It was almost as if poor old Gregory had been waiting in the wings to snap up Brittany as soon as she was available. And clearly Brittany hadn't minded.

"You're right," Nick agreed, amazement lining his voice. He didn't know how he hadn't seen it before, but lately he seemed to have been blind about a lot of things. "And I wish the two of them well."

He was just happy it wasn't him.

"As do I," she said, chuckling at his expression. "But you do realize that in your quest to redeem yourself with the town, you *have*, however unintentionally, made it look like we are more than simple business associates."

He had. He knew he had. And it hadn't been entirely unintentional. He knew it was a bad idea. He had too many responsibilities to even consider a relationship right now. He'd only end up letting his girlfriend down, like he'd done with Brittany. And with Vivian laser-focused on starting up her business—not to mention whatever drama had happened with her baby's father—he doubted she was looking for love, either.

Yet he couldn't seem to stop himself from getting closer to her. He enjoyed being around Vivian, whether it was strolling through the park, laughing at her blaring orange Broncos jersey or even shoveling cow patties out of her shop.

Without consciously meaning to, he had set off down the very path he had promised himself he would never go down again.

He was starting to have feelings for her.

This couldn't happen. He needed to nip this in the bud. Immediately. Before he messed things up and hurt Vivian. It was only a matter of time.

"I'm thinking I'm not cut out to be a family man."

There. That should do it.

"Because of one bad relationship?" She scoffed and waved him off, though he noticed the pain that flashed through her eyes. "Don't be silly."

He snorted. "Believe me, it's been more than one. Brittany is, unfortunately for the women of Serendipity, just the last and most vocal of my long string of failures."

"You're being too hard on yourself."

"Am I?" He looked deep into her eyes, seeing warmth, enthusiasm and…*belief*. Belief in him. Confidence in the man he could become.

Trust.

If her gentle smile was anything to go by, she clearly wasn't going to let him get away with judging himself too harshly.

"Who knows?" Her blue eyes glittered with amusement. "Maybe you just haven't met the right woman yet."

Her bright smile almost convinced him that her words were true and that she believed them. But there was too much she wasn't telling him.

"Do you really believe that, or does this rule only apply to me?" he asked gently.

Her gaze dropped to her belly and she refused to look up at him.

"You've got me," she said on a sigh. "I'm really good at giving other people advice, but I'm not so good at taking my own."

"Meaning?" He reached for her hand and covered it with his.

"Does it not bother you that you're hanging around with a pregnant single woman? Do you not wonder if I'm being hypocritical, attending church as an unwed mother?"

He immediately shook his head. He didn't. He never had. Whatever Viv's story turned out to be, he had no doubt that she was a genuine woman of faith.

"Well, I am a hypocrite. Or at least, I was." She blew out a breath.

"You don't have to tell me this if you don't want to."

"No, I think I do."

He nodded for her to continue.

After a long pause, she spoke again. "I was engaged to Derrick—the father of my son. I'm ashamed to admit I allowed myself to be pulled into a verbally and emotionally abusive relationship."

His hand tightened around hers. Without knowing one more detail about this Derrick guy, Nick wanted to throttle him. That wouldn't help Vivian or her baby now, but he wished he could have protected Vivian from such a cad.

"Derrick put a lot of pressure on me to turn my back on my faith, on my morals. But I can't lay all the blame at his door. In the end it was my bad decision and wrong actions."

"You got pregnant."

"Yes." She laid a protective hand over her belly. "I knew it was wrong, what Derrick and I had done, but I truly believed it would all work out in the end. I thought we would get married, just sooner than we'd planned. But when I told Derrick about the baby, he was furious. Even though he knew perfectly well he was the only man I'd ever been with, he denied he was the father and declared he wanted nothing to do with either one of us."

Nick had a hard time believing any man could be so cruel. Any *real* man. Derrick definitely wouldn't qualify for that category.

"Has he contacted you since?"

"No. I've called him a few times, but he recently changed his phone number. I'm truly on my own."

Nick tipped her chin up so she had no choice but to meet his gaze.

"No, you're not," he whispered, his voice gravelly. "You're not alone."

Chapter Six

"Uncle Nick! Uncle Nick!"

Vivian laughed as young Brody, Slade's adopted four-year-old son, launched himself into Nick's arms. In Brody's exuberance, he overshot his mark and nearly barreled into Vivian.

Her pulse jumped up and she placed a protective hand over her middle. It was only Nick's quick reflexes that kept her from being wrestled right off the park bench.

Nick leaned in to catch Brody, swinging him into the air and wiggling him until he giggled in delight. The black-and-white-spotted ball the boy had been holding dropped to the ground, unnoticed.

"Look where you're going, little dude," Nick said, setting the boy on his feet again.

"You nearly knocked over this pretty young lady here."

Vivian's heart skipped a beat. Did he really think she was pretty? Did that mean he didn't see her as damaged or flawed, even after all she'd just told him?

"It's nothing," she assured them.

"Yes, it is," Nick contended. "In the McKenna family little men learn to be courteous to ladies. And that includes not knocking them off of park benches. Especially not women about to have a baby. We have to be extra respectful of them."

Vivian had a sudden vision of being cradled in Nick's arms the day she'd fallen over the drywall. He'd been so afraid she'd hurt herself. At the time all she could remember was feeling annoyed, but now the memory came along with sensory details, things she'd missed the first time.

The gentleness and worry lining his deep, rich voice. The scent of leather and spice that was uniquely Nick. The rippling of the muscles in his arms and chest. The way he carried her as if she weighed no more than a feather, even though her body had thickened with her unborn child.

"Brody, you have to treat girls with respect. You have to be nice to them."

Brody made a face and reached for his ball. Evidently he wasn't a big fan of girls yet.

"What do you say you apologize to Miss Vivian?" Nick gently took the boy's shoulders and turned him toward her.

Little Brody's head hung. He looked adorably contrite. "Sorry I almost hit you," he muttered almost too quietly to hear.

"You are quite forgiven, sweetheart. No hard feelings, okay?" She reached out a hand to the boy and they shook on it.

Nick stole the ball from Brody's grip. He hefted the ball back to Brody and grinned at Viv. "Do you mind if I play with my nephew for a few?"

"No, not at all. Take your time. After spending the whole morning with a mask over my face, I'm enjoying the fresh air. Have fun playing with your basketball."

Brody crowed with laughter.

"It's a soccer ball," Nick corrected, one corner of his lips tugging up.

"You kick the ball, not bounce it," Brody informed her in a solemn tone of voice.

"I apologize for my mistake," Viv said

with equal seriousness. "I'm a complete new-bie where sports are concerned. I promise I will remember that fact for the next time I observe soccer."

Nick winked at her and lobbed the ball out onto the green grass. Both Nick and Brody chased after it, hooting and hollering as they kicked it back and forth to each other.

Vivian waved to Laney, who was sitting under a shelter chatting with a group of women and then turned her attention back to the boys. She thought the game itself was as boring as watching oil dry. Kicking the ball back and forth, back and forth, with no end in sight. But she enjoyed watching Nick interact with his nephew.

Nick's expression, usually so serious, re-laxed, the hard ridges and lines of stress diminishing. Rich laughter bubbled from his chest as he feigned right, then left, and then let little Brody steal the ball away from him—all without letting the boy know that Nick was giving rather than taking.

She loved watching how Nick subtly raised the child's confidence as he taught him how to move the ball—dribble…apparently the word was *dribble*—across the grass using only the insides of his feet.

Considering the fact that they'd both admonished her that soccer was all about *kicking* the ball, it seemed to her that they spent an awful lot of time bouncing the ball off of other body parts—in particular, their heads.

At one point, Nick even picked the ball off the ground and tossed it repeatedly at Brody so the boy could practice popping the ball into the air with his forehead.

What kind of barbarity was that? What was he trying to do? Give the poor little dude brain damage?

Men. And little men. It was easy for Vivian to believe they might well be an entirely different species. Would it be the same way with her son? How could she ever hope to keep up with Baby G if she didn't understand the way he ticked?

If it was anybody but Nick, she would have worried about Brody getting hurt, but his affection for his nephew was obvious in Nick's every move, head-bonking notwithstanding. His encouragement was visibly raising the boy's confidence level in addition to his skill on the playing field.

And he thought he wasn't cut out to be a family man? Anyone with eyes in their head could see how good he was with children. How could he not see that in himself?

Nick smiled and waved at her, and for the first time in her life, she wished she'd paid more attention to sports when she was in school so she could join Nick and Brody in their play. She'd attended a few games in high school, but she had always been too busy talking with her friends to pay any attention to what was happening on the field. And she'd hated phys ed.

Who would teach her son how to dribble a soccer ball, or even pop it off his forehead, though the thought made her cringe? She certainly wouldn't be the one to do it.

Here she was, in a park full of happy, joy-filled adults and children, and she felt the most completely and utterly alone she'd ever been. Her baby's future, his care and his happiness, all depended on her. She had no partner in life with whom to share both the blessings and the burdens of parenthood.

It was she and she alone.

How could she possibly teach her son all the things he'd need to know to grow into adulthood? How could she be both mother and father to him? She didn't even know the difference between a basketball and a soccer ball, much less how to play the games. It was a silly thing, she knew, but at the moment it felt totally overwhelming.

She was long past being angry that Derrick had abandoned her, but she still couldn't comprehend how he could possibly refuse to be a father to his own son, or even to acknowledge paternity.

Deep down, Viv knew that it was the best thing for both her and her child. What kind of father would Derrick have made anyway, moving in and out of their son's life? He wouldn't have given the baby any stability or security.

Not to mention, Derrick hadn't treated her well, and she doubted he would have been any better with their baby. It was by God's grace that she had gotten out of that toxic relationship and returned to Serendipity where she belonged. She couldn't bear the thought of her precious baby exposed to that kind of abuse. But even though in her heart she knew it would have been detrimental to have had Derrick in their lives, it still didn't seem fair that her child had to grow up in a single-parent household—especially hers.

She felt so completely inadequate for the

task. A child deserved to grow up with a mother and a father.

In a perfect world.

She didn't realize Nick and Brody had stopped kicking the ball around until Nick suddenly dropped onto the bench beside her, his breath coming in short, shallow gasps. Sweat slicked his forehead and he used the bottom of his T-shirt to dab it away.

"Brody, you need to take it easy on your poor uncle Nick," Nick said, grabbing the boy around the shoulders and tickling his belly. "I'm too old to keep up with you."

Nick met Viv's gaze and raised his eyebrows, clearly expecting a laugh. She really should be laughing.

Nick, an out-of-shape old man?

Laughable.

She managed to wrestle up a smile but couldn't summon the mirth to go with it, even when Nick lagged his tongue out to the side and panted like a pooch.

"You goof," she said, playfully shoving his shoulder. She appreciated what he was doing to get her out of her funk, even if it wasn't working.

He narrowed his gaze on her and then reached out and gently caressed the line of her jaw. A million tiny electrical currents accompanied the slow path of his fingertips.

"You usually think so." He leaned forward until his lips were mere centimeters from her ear. His warm breath fanned her cheeks, sending a shiver of awareness down her spine.

"What's wrong?" he whispered.

"It's nothing." She nodded toward Brody.

"Right. Hey, dude, you'd better go check in with your mom." He waved at Laney as Brody darted across the park to return to her side.

With Brody safe with Laney, Nick turned his full attention on Vivian. "Are you feeling all right? Is your morning sickness bothering you?"

Did she look nauseated? If she did, it was all Derrick's fault. Just the thought of him was now enough to turn her stomach. But she was tired of thinking about him. He was no longer a part of her life and she didn't want to waste any more brain cells or emotional energy wondering about him.

She placed a palm over her belly. She'd been feeling tiny little butterfly flutters for a couple of weeks now, but this time she felt definite movement under her hand.

She gasped.

Nick's brow lowered. "Should I call 9-1-1?"

After all of the conflicting emotions she'd experienced over the past hour, the thought of Nick calling 9-1-1 because he thought she might be experiencing morning sickness was too much for her.

She didn't know whether to laugh or cry, so she did both. She chuckled and hiccupped simultaneously and then tears of joy sprang to her eyes.

All of her anxiety dissipated. Her problems appeared minute compared to the magnitude of the joy of feeling new life moving within her.

She wasn't alone. She carried Baby G under her heart. Soon she would be holding her precious newborn in her arms. There was nothing but God's blessing in that.

And she had Nick hovering anxiously over her, looking as if he was about ready to jump out of his skin. It warmed her heart to see him act that way. Even though he had no vested interest in them, he was overtly protective of her and her baby.

"I just felt him move," she explained, her voice cracking with emotion.

Nick's large blue eyes filled with wonder.

"I've been feeling flutters for a couple of weeks now, but this is the first time I've felt a good, solid kick."

Nick chuckled. "Baby G probably wanted to join Brody and me in our soccer game."

"That must be it," she agreed, joining in his laughter. "I guess I'd better start learning the rules of the game.

"Oh!" She reached for Nick's hand and placed it on the side of her swollen belly. "There he is again. Can you feel him? I think it's his heel."

As if in answer to her question, the baby moved again. Vivian thought he might have done a full backflip this time, the little show-off.

Nick's smile couldn't have been any wider and his gaze shone with delight. "I did. I felt him move. It's amazing. What a blessing you've got there."

Her hand tightened over his and she swallowed hard against the tumult of emotions welling inside her.

Now that he'd gotten their attention, Baby G appeared to be doing gymnastics.

Nick chortled. "I think he's showing off for his uncle Nick."

Uncle Nick?

Her heart skipped and then charged into beating double-time.

Maybe her son *would* have a solid, trustworthy male role model in his life, after all. She'd assumed once the spa was finished, her association with Nick would end.

She was exhilarated to hear that she was wrong.

And if Nick intended to be involved with her baby—what did that mean for the two of them?

She was afraid to even begin to consider the implications, but they nonetheless nestled someplace deep in her heart.

She offered up a silent prayer. She wasn't alone.

Though a manager had been hired in October and residents had been trickling in for weeks, Thanksgiving Day marked the official grand opening of Serendipity's senior center. It seemed only right to celebrate such a momentous occasion on the day set aside for giving thanks.

Nick finished a family meal with his mother, Jax—along with his new fiancée, Faith, and his adorable, twin baby girls—and

Slade and Laney with Brody. After a relaxed dinner filled with good food and great fellowship, Nick and his mother headed out to watch the town council cut the red ribbon and invite the public to see the results of their generosity at the auction.

As with the rest of his family, Nick was anxious to see how his uncle James was settling in to his new home.

But along with this successful grand opening, Nick was mulling over other plans, ones that had gone awry, not at all as hoped or expected. Despite the fact that he'd spent every spare minute at Viv's shop, they hadn't been able to open the doors to the salon and spa in time for the holidays the way she'd planned.

Vivian hadn't said anything—she always kept her chin up and her attitude positive—but he knew the burden of stress she was shouldering, and it had to be overwhelming.

She was the bravest, most stalwart woman he'd ever known, but he worried about her, and he was concerned about the baby. Once the town had found out about her condition, his mother had encouraged him to watch over Vivian, informing him that undue stress could send a woman into premature labor. Nick wasn't sure how he could help, other than to do what he was already doing—taking care of as many details regarding the spa as possible and surreptitiously trying to make sure she took care of herself.

He felt woefully inadequate. But what else was he supposed to do? Though she denied it, he knew it was more than just her business affairs that were bothering her. Ever since that day in the park, she'd been more withdrawn and introspective.

Something was different. Something had changed. He hoped it had nothing to do with this Derrick fellow, but he couldn't be sure.

Unless she chose to open up to him and talk about her problems, he was powerless to help her.

He'd told her the truth about what had happened between him and Brittany and had come clean about the agenda he'd created after Vivian won him in the auction.

Had those confessions led to Viv having second thoughts about working with him? He wouldn't be surprised. Why should she trust him, a man who had consistently proven himself untrustworthy? His past was catching up with him, rushing in on him, coloring his future.

Lord, make me a new man.

It was more than just changing his behavior. Change had to come from his heart. And, he acknowledged, as he watched old Frank Spencer, Jo's husband and the president of the town council, cut the ribbon to the senior center, only God could transform a man's heart and make the old man new again.

Nick prayed the Lord would bless him, that he would find the much longed-for peace, and that he could somehow then pass it on to Vivian and her baby.

He tucked his mother's hand into the crook of his arm as the crowd jostled their way into the new center. The facility was set up into two wings—one side for active seniors who needed little more than an occasional check-in, while the other side was a long-term care ward which provided around-the-clock care for folks like Uncle James. At the hub of the two wards was the main office, the cafeteria and a large common area with two television sets and a variety of reading material and board games.

As they entered the center, Nick kept a discreet eye out for Vivian, but he didn't see her anywhere, although her twin sister, Alexis, was hosting the bake sale.

"Do you want to go and see if we can find Uncle James?" Nick asked his mother.

Alice patted his shoulder. "You go on ahead, dear. I'll catch up with you in a minute."

A group of Alice's friends from church were waving her over. His mom didn't get out as much socially as she'd used to before Nick's dad had died, but helping Jax with his twin babies had put a bit of a spring back into her step—as had the announcement of Jax's engagement to Faith, who Alice doted on. Nick was glad to see she'd begun embracing life again and reconnecting with her friends.

Sometimes, like now, being a large man in a tight space with a lot of people was more of a detriment than a help, and it took him a while to make his way through the crowd to the corridor leading to the long-term care ward.

He wasn't sure what kind of condition he'd find Uncle James in today. Some days the man was entirely lucid. On other days, he had no idea who Nick was, and even on occasion became frightened or aggressive in Nick's presence.

His own father had been the same way near the end. Nick had never been entirely comfortable with Jenson's illness, and deep down he wondered if that was part of the reason he hadn't been there when his dad passed. Had he used the ranch to avoid emotions he'd rather not confront?

Nick wasn't the same man now. He was committed to making regular visits to his uncle James, whether or not the man was aware he was there.

He was looking for his uncle's apartment when he suddenly heard a soft, high tinkle of laughter coming from a nearby room. The sound reminded him of a fairy.

He knew that laugh.

He peeked into the room where he'd heard Viv's laughter and stopped short, his breath catching in his throat.

She was sitting between two old ladies, and the three of them were chatting and giggling like schoolgirls. Nick didn't think either of the women knew who Viv was—maybe they didn't even know who they were, themselves. They both had dementia's blank-eyed stare, and yet Vivian had them fully engaged as she painted their fingernails a glistening bright red.

Vivian didn't look the least bit uncomfortable with the old women. Nick knew that in their minds, Vivian might be a long-lost daughter or granddaughter, or an old friend rather than just a kind stranger, but they were clearly enjoying her ministrations.

As Viv stretched the small of her back, she glanced up and met Nick's gaze as he stood in the doorway. She extended her hand and her sunny smile to him.

"Well, don't just stand there, Nick. Come on in and let me introduce you to these two lovely ladies. This is Opal," she said, gesturing to the woman on the right. "And this is Marjorie. They share this suite."

Nick grinned and tipped his hat to the ladies. "Nice to meet you both."

"Nick here is doing all the carpentry on the beauty salon I've been telling you about. He's doing a lovely job. I'm so pleased with the outcome."

Pride swelled in Nick's chest. He usually had women yelling at him, not praising him. It felt mighty fine.

Her kind words made him want to earn Vivian's respect even more.

"Are you all related?" he asked.

"They're sisters," Viv answered. "But I'm no relation to them. I'm just floating around here today offering my services to all of the residents. Primping hair and painting finger-nails and toenails for the ladies. Shaves and haircuts for any of the guys who want it."

She gave him a once-over that made his nerves tingle. He didn't like the look in her eye, nor the fact that she had shears and a razor in her apron.

"Your husband is a real looker." Marjorie gestured toward Nick.

"Yes, but he's unkempt," Opal added frankly. "You really should do something about that hair, Viv."

"Oh, I'm not—" Nick started to say, but Vivian cut him off with the briefest shake of her head.

She was right, of course. The women would probably just get confused if he tried to explain that he and Viv weren't married. The old folks saw what they wanted to see.

"I know, right?" she said instead. "He won't let me anywhere near him with a pair of scissors. I'm going to keep trying, though."

Gathering her supplies, she kissed each of the ladies on the cheek and reached for Nick's elbow, guiding him out of the room.

He stopped just outside the door.

"They thought we were—"

"I know," she said, smothering a chuckle. "Can you imagine?"

Their eyes met and held, and for one moment, as he lost himself in the impossibly deep blue pools of her eyes, Nick *could* imagine. His pulse jolted to life and his gaze dropped to her lips.

She laughed nervously and turned away from him, gesturing to a room across the hallway.

"Were you looking for your uncle? I believe that's his apartment over there."

It took Nick a beat to regroup. He glanced at the door number and nodded. "Yep. That's him."

"Does he need his hair cut, do you think?"

"I doubt it. He usually keeps his hair shaved into a buzz cut."

She produced a pair of shears from her apron pocket and waved them at him in mock menace.

"How about you? What do you say, Nick? Are you ready for a haircut and a nice close shave?"

He belted out a laugh and held both hands up in protest. "You stay away from me with those things."

"Spoilsport." She pouted playfully, her full

lips arcing downward. "Just think of what good advertising you would be for my salon."

He shook his head. "No, ma'am. Your beauty salon doesn't need my kind of advertising. That would be catastrophic—especially since it isn't even open yet."

A shadow crossed her gaze and he wanted to kick himself.

Way to go, McKenna. Remind her of all the hurdles they still had to jump over to get her spa up and running.

He reached for her free hand—the one without a sharp instrument in it.

"It'll happen, Vivian," he promised. "Maybe not on our original timetable, but your spa *will* open, and it will be successful. Wait and see. Remember, it's all in God's hands, sweetheart."

"I know," she said through tight lips.

She didn't sound like she believed him. It was discouraging, his Vivian losing faith.

His Vivian? Now, where had that come from?

"Nick? Is that you?" Uncle James appeared in the doorway in a battered brown bathrobe and mismatched house shoes. "I thought it was your voice I heard."

"Hello, Mr. McKenna," Vivian said brightly,

all traces of her own worries instantly erased as she addressed the man. "Are you settling in okay?"

James stared at her, suddenly confused. "Who are you?"

Vivian's smile didn't waver. "My name's Vivian."

"Viv's a friend of mine, Uncle James."

James seemed to dismiss her, his gaze fixed back on Nick. "Are you here to take me home?"

Nick swallowed hard. How could he explain to his uncle that this *was* home?

He looked to Vivian for guidance. She was way better at dealing with people than he was. She flashed him an encouraging smile.

"Do you have any treats in that minifridge of yours?" she asked, diverting his uncle's thoughts. "Nick hasn't eaten in at least an hour. I'm sure he's famished."

She glanced back at Nick and winked, her lips twitching with mirth.

He nodded, acknowledging both her sense of humor and his thanks.

"Come on, Uncle James," he said, gently turning his uncle by the shoulders and leading him back into the room.

"I'll stop by the cafeteria and see what

they've got for you," Viv volunteered. "But then I've got to get back to the other residents. There are a lot of ladies waiting to get their hair done."

He watched her walk away, marveling at her ability to give of herself to others even when she was struggling through issues in her own life.

Not every woman had such a large and loving heart.

But then again, not every woman was Vivian Grainger.

Chapter Seven

⟨⟩

Three weeks before Christmas, with the holiday season in full swing, Vivian found herself busier than ever. Now in her third trimester, she felt like someone had strapped a giant watermelon onto her body, but thankfully the morning sickness was long behind her and her energy level was at its peak.

Baby G was more active with every day that passed, although he was growing so big he had a lot less room to move within her. She was a little short on sleep because her son apparently believed her rest time was his playtime. Sometimes it felt like he was using her ribs as monkey bars, but she gloried in every movement. She couldn't wait to meet her sweet little one face-to-face and hold him in her arms.

Not long now. Her due date was only a few weeks away, about a week into the New Year.

In the meantime, she had plenty to keep her mind and hands occupied. She volunteered at the senior center twice a week, keeping the residents happily curled and manicured.

Once she'd passed Thanksgiving, she'd accepted both rationally and emotionally the fact that it was going to take her longer than she'd originally hoped and anticipated to open the spa.

Deciding on a new grand-opening date had been problematic, since she had to take into account that Baby G was soon to make his debut into the world. It would be difficult, but not impossible. She would open her salon, have her baby and take a two-week maternity leave before returning to work.

As for the building itself, things were finally falling into place. The electrical system was correctly rewired, the plumbing issues were fixed, and the inspector would make final rounds with Nick on Wednesday.

All new styling chairs had been installed, as had the massage chairs for pedicures. She had a massage table for use with guests looking for a deep tissue massage.

A beautiful walnut desk and file cabinet

now graced her office. She'd hired her staff, two young ladies with recently obtained cosmetology and massage licenses who were excited to begin their careers at Viv's salon. She was glad she could hire locally and contribute to Serendipity's economy.

And she'd finally settled on a name for her new business.

Tranquility.

A name that she hoped she could live up to, that she could really offer her clientele. Maybe she'd even eventually find some of that peace for herself.

She prayed she'd be able to have the salon open for at least a week or two before her baby came. She wanted to be there to make sure the grand opening went off as designed and everything in the salon was working smoothly. Still, to be on the safe side, she'd taken the time to create a contingency plan and was confident the two girls could hold down the fort until she could get back to work after the baby was born.

It wasn't ideal by any means, but with Nick's help with the remodel and the young cosmetologists ready to take over when the baby was born, it could be done.

It had to be. She couldn't afford to wait

much longer before the salon started bringing in revenue.

Today, though, she would put her apprehensions about the opening of Tranquility aside.

The senior center was throwing its highly anticipated, first annual Christmas party. Decorations, food and fellowship, brought from the townsfolk's hearts to the beloved elderly population in their care.

Christmas was by far Vivian's favorite time of year, when everyone's attention turned toward the infant Jesus, when hearts and minds were filled with an attitude of joy and giving. Peace on earth, goodwill toward man. Evergreen trees and lights on all the houses. Candles lit in the darkened sanctuary of the church for the midnight service. The children's pageant, which was always adorable and often amusing.

It warmed her heart to think that in just a few years, her son would take part in the pageant—playing the part of a sheep or a donkey, perhaps. He would be the cutest kid in the pageant, whatever his role—and he would have the proudest mama.

She laughed at herself as she entered the senior center facility, her arms laden with rolls of sparkling garland in several colors, with which she would help decorate for the festivities. She was definitely getting ahead of herself. Her son needed to be born before he could participate in the nativity play.

Alexis, Griff, Jo Spencer and a half a dozen others were gathered in the commons area, digging through bins overflowing with glittering ball ornaments, tinsel and strings of colorful lights that had been donated to the senior center. An enormous Virginia pine tree was set up in the middle of the room, waiting to be trimmed.

"Late, as usual," Alexis teased as Vivian dumped her armful of garland next to the other decorations.

"Better late than later," she quipped back, knowing even as she said the words that her maxim wasn't quite right.

Thankfully, Nick wasn't there to correct her, and everyone else just let it go. The saying, whatever it was, could apply to her salon as well as her habitual lateness, a personal trait she had tried but failed to amend over the years.

"I see you haven't had any success cleaning Nick up. Are you ready to do *my* laundry for two months?"

"I'm not out of time yet. The salon's official grand opening isn't until next week."

"I prefer liquid fabric softener in the washing machine as opposed to the dryer sheets you use."

Vivian made a face at her twin, knowing it was entirely possible that she *would* be doing double duty on laundry soon. Up until now Nick hadn't budged on the whole haircut-and-a-shave thing. She doubted she was going to get him to change his mind in the next week.

"Okay, folks," Jo said, taking charge as usual. "We need a game plan here. The tree needs trimming. Griff and Alexis, why don't you take care of that task. I need a few of you to *deck the halls* with garland, tinsel and evergreen wreaths."

She paused and tapped her chin. "Now, we need a little bit of a North Pole flavor in that corner over there. We'll have to to get creative and make a sleigh with the trimmings we have here in the bins, but we've got a reindeer, thanks to Nick McKenna. Vivian, why don't you and Nick work on that together."

"But Nick is—"

"Even later than you are, for once," Nick said from behind her left shoulder.

Startled by his voice, her heart leaped into her throat. She placed a hand on her pounding chest to even her breathing.

"Your bad habits are rubbing off on me," he teased.

"I beg your pardon," she said, whirling on him, only to nearly crash into the life-size, one-dimensional wooden cutout of a reindeer.

"I've got Dasher," he informed her, moving the reindeer up and down to simulate flying. "Dancer, Prancer and the rest of the lot couldn't make it today."

"Did you carve that? It's pretty intricate. I've got to say, I'm impressed."

Nick nodded. "I drew the pattern myself."

He was clearly pleased with her praise. She thought his chest might have ballooned a bit and he was standing a good inch taller.

"What are we going to do for a sleigh?" Viv asked as they sifted through the decorations in the bins, looking for ideas to create the North Pole.

"What about this?" Nick asked, holding up a large tablecloth, which was a bright red trimmed with green around the edges. "We can push a couple of folding chairs together and drape this over them."

Vivian caught his enthusiasm. "We can use some gold garland for the reins. And here's a bag of fake snow. It'll be a mess to clean up but it'll definitely give us the ambiance we're looking for. Oh—and we can wrap red ribbon around that concrete pole over there to make it look like a giant candy cane."

Nick chuckled. "The North Pole. Nice."

For the next half hour Vivian and Nick built the scene in the corner of the commons. Nick set up his reindeer and wrapped the pole in red ribbon, while Vivian worked on the sleigh and spread glistening fake snow across the floor around their display.

"We should see if we can find a couple of large, empty boxes," Vivian suggested as they stood back and examined the scene they'd created. "I've got an extra roll of wrapping paper in my car."

"I like that idea. We can stack the fake presents next to the sleigh."

Their gazes met and Vivian smiled up at him. "Now all we need is Santa."

Nick shifted his gaze away from her to where Alexis was trimming the tree. "It looks like your sister is about finished."

"The tree is beautiful. I love the twinkling lights. They bring such peace to my heart."

"Hey, Nick, can I get your help over here?" Alexis asked, waving him over.

"Sure. The tree looks great, by the way. What do you need me to do?"

"Put the angel on. I'm not tall enough to reach the top of the tree and Jo shanghaied Griff into helping decorate the cafeteria."

"Not a problem," he said, picking up the angel—a sweet, smiling figure robed in white with gold trim. But then, with a wink and a smile, he immediately turned to Vivian and placed the angel in her hands.

That made less than no sense. If Alexis couldn't reach the top of the tree, then Vivian would fare no better. They were identical twins, after all.

"Up we go," Nick said, hoisting her into the air before she even knew what he was going to do.

"Nick, you can't—" she started to protest, but then realized it would do no good. He could, apparently, and he did. He'd quite literally swept her off her feet on more than one occasion.

Of course, now she was over eight months pregnant, so it was a little bit awkward.

"Are you going to make me stand here

holding you all day or are you going to put the angel on the top of the tree?" Nick asked.

She put the angel on the top of the tree.

"There, now," he said, gently setting her back on her feet and holding her waist firmly until he was certain she was stable. "My family has an old Christmas tradition. Prettiest girl gets to top the tree."

Vivian rolled her eyes and pointed out the obvious weakness in his statement. "You have two brothers."

He grinned. "Okay, you got me. Our tradition is that the youngest member of the family tops the tree. It was Brody this year, since Jax's twins aren't quite old enough to grasp the concept of Christmas. Or trees. Still, all things being even, I like my idea better."

"You do realize that my identical twin is standing right here next to me."

"So I'm surrounded by two beautiful women. It's a really tough situation for a guy to be in, but I'll try to bear it. And I'm standing firm on what I said. The prettiest girl got to top the tree."

Vivian's face grew warm. Alexis was beaming at her, clearly not at all offended by Nick's declaration. Her eyes were glittering with amusement.

Nick looked like the cat who caught the parakeet.

"Besides," Nick added, "technically, the youngest person did top the tree. You had Baby G's help, didn't you?"

She couldn't help but laugh.

"Festivities are about to begin, people," Jo declared, clapping her hands to get everyone's attention. "Let's get these bins put away so we can all join the *p-a-r-t-y*. Party!"

What a card Jo was, parading around in her green T-shirt that proclaimed Elfette and her matching green hat that contrasted with the brassy red curls of her hair.

Vivian grabbed one of the bins and followed the others to the storage closet, where they neatly stacked everything away out of sight. She'd thought Nick was right behind her, but when she turned to speak to him about wrapping some empty boxes, she discovered he wasn't there. Strange. Maybe he'd been held back in the commons area for some reason.

She decided she'd have to see to the fake presents herself. She found a couple of empty boxes in the storage closet and made a quick detour to her car, where she wrapped them in foiled paper.

By the time she returned to the commons area, it was filled with senior residents and their families, along with a smattering of nurses. She looked around for Nick but he was nowhere to be seen.

She also didn't see his uncle. Maybe Nick had gone to fetch James and accompany him to the party.

She stacked the presents next to the sleigh and then made her way over to the punch bowl. She sipped at a cup of hot apple cider, content for the moment just to watch folks interacting with each other. The nurses that had relocated to the area to accompany some of the frailer residents moving in from surrounding towns were welcomed like family. The folks in Serendipity were like that.

Vivian's heart warmed. She felt blessed to live here, to be back home again where she belonged. Whatever happened in the future, she had this.

What more could a woman want?

She didn't want to answer that. Not today.

She set her empty mug on a nearby tray and was just about to start mingling when Jo caught her by the elbow and shoved a black point-and-click camera into her hand.

"We're about to start, dear. Would you mind taking pictures?"

Start?

Vivian thought the party had started a while ago. Was Jo talking about something else? But what else was there?

The buzz of conversation dissipated as everyone turned their attention to the corner where Vivian and Nick had set up their display.

She couldn't really see what was happening through the crowd of people, and from this vantage point, she definitely wouldn't be able to take any pictures of whatever was going on.

She was making her way through the crowd and had just reached the beribboned North Pole when she heard Nick's deep, rich voice, loud and clear.

"Ho, ho, ho. Merry Christmas!"

Nick caught one glimpse of Vivian's startled face and knew it had been worth whatever discomfort he was feeling from wearing this thick, itchy red suit. He didn't have much time to enjoy her reaction before she raised the camera she'd been holding and the flash went off, temporarily blinding him.

He should have expected that. It was actually his camera that Nick had given Jo, telling her to pass it on to Vivian. It wasn't so much that he wanted to be able to see a picture of himself in the Santa getup as it was making sure Viv was there when he made his entrance.

He knew she'd be amused by the prospect, probably even more than his brothers, but he had to admit he kind of liked it when she teased him.

How he had been talked into playing this role in the first place he would never understand. He was the last man on the planet anyone would expect to dress up as Santa Claus. Yet one day when Nick was visiting his uncle, the center's facility manager approached him and told him Jo had suggested asking him if he'd mind playing Old Saint Nick for the seniors at the center.

Mind?

Of course he minded. He might have the right name, but that was the only thing he had in common with the jolly old elf.

Christmas spirit wasn't exactly his forte.

But then he'd thought about Vivian, who regularly and selflessly offered her services to the residents of the care center. He knew the elderly here would revel in a visit from Santa.

And so he had said yes.

Everyone's eyes were turned on him, making his skin prickle. The red suit was itchy, the pillow he'd stuffed down the front of his coat kept shifting awkwardly and when he went to sit down on the makeshift sleigh, the chairs beneath him shifted apart and the reindeer he'd spent countless hours constructing nearly capsized.

Carefully adjusting his weight so his "sleigh" would remain stable and he wouldn't slip between the chairs, he set down his pack filled with gifts for the residents and wondered what he was supposed to do next. He hadn't been given a script, and it wasn't like the elderly were going to come sit on his lap and tell him what they wanted for Christmas.

Were they?

The thought made him chuckle, which he quickly masked as the loud, hearty laugh of the character he was supposed to be playing.

Deciding there was no reason to linger any longer than strictly necessary, it appeared the obvious thing to do would be to pass out the gifts. He was anxious to wrap this up and get out of the torturous Santa suit. Anything he could do to move things along would be a blessing.

He reached for the bag, but before he could pull out the first gift, he was stopped by his brother Jax, who slid one of his infant girls—Nick's niece—into Nick's arm and a family-sized black leather Bible, its pages gilded with gold trim, into the other hand.

Nick raised his white-powdered brow. "What, exactly, am I supposed to do with these?" he whispered raggedly.

Jax scoffed and shook his head. "I should think that would be obvious. I have the Bible bookmarked to the second chapter of Luke. Read the gospel story about the nativity of our Lord. And Violet here," Jax said with a grin, "is your special effects team. Don't worry. She's my mellow baby."

"I can't read aloud to a crowd of people." Nick was panicking and almost started to hyperventilate. He'd always been a poor reader and struggled with dyslexia. He would never be able to do a Bible story justice, especially one as holy as the birth of Christ.

Jax clapped his shoulder. "I believe in you, bro."

"Let me help you with this." Nick was so focused on trying to drag a breath through his closed throat that he hadn't even noticed Vivian approaching.

She took the Bible from him and relief rippled through his tense muscles. With her outgoing personality, he was sure Vivian excelled in front of crowds. He was certain she would do a bang-up job reading the Christmas story.

She opened the Holy Scriptures and removed the ribbon bookmark, and then promptly handed it back to Nick with a sunny smile.

"There you are. I figured the Bible would be difficult to open, seeing as you have a baby in your other arm."

"Opening the Bible wasn't my big concern," he muttered, but she was already crouched before him, watching him intently, waiting for him to start reading.

Way to force the issue. Folks had settled down in chairs or on the floor and the room was filled with silent expectation. Even baby Violet appeared to be staring up at Nick in anticipation of the story.

Santa suit. Seniors. Bible. Baby.

He couldn't get out of it now.

He cleared his throat and concentrated on the words before him.

"In those days a decree went out from Caesar Augustus…"

The first few sentences were a little rough, but then he fell into his role and got caught up in the story. He must have heard it a hundred times over the years, but it never grew old, remembering the story of God coming to earth as Man. Nick all gussied up as Santa Claus as he read the story represented it in a whole new way. Kind of choked him up.

"That was beautiful," Vivian breathed when the last word was spoken.

"Indeed," said Jo, who added applause for his efforts to her comment. "Well done!" The rest of the crowd joined in the applause.

He nodded, acknowledging the residents and their families. With a tender touch, Jax gently transferred Violet back into his own arms. Nick winked at his brother. Jax had certainly taken to fatherhood well, especially considering the fact that his twins had been literally dumped on his doorstep five months ago.

"Good job, bro," Jax said. "I'm proud of you."

"Back at ya," Nick said, refusing to acknowledge the swell in his chest. He wasn't usually so emotional.

"Are we ready for some gift giving?" Jo announced in a voice loud enough to penetrate the room.

Nick handed the Bible to Vivian and she set it aside.

"I'm as ready as a man can be," he whispered, for Viv's ears only. "I am so itching to get out of this ridiculous suit."

She giggled and patted the pillow on his stomach. "I think you look cute."

Cute?

Heat flooded to his face. It was a good thing Santa Claus was supposed to have rosy cheeks, because he knew his were flaming.

Without him having to ask, Vivian positioned herself next to the sack of gifts and handed carefully wrapped gifts to him one at a time, allowing him to have the fun of passing them out to the seniors.

"That's a lot of wrapping," he commented to Viv as he pressed a package into an old woman's hands.

"You're telling me," Vivian said with a laugh. "It took Alexis and me an entire day to get them all done."

"You and Alexis wrapped *all* these gifts?"

She sniffed. "Don't sound so surprised. I

am capable of wrapping Christmas presents, you know."

"I didn't mean it that way. I just meant that it's incredible that you put that much effort into it."

She smiled softly. "It's worth it. Look at all these happy faces."

And there were. The seniors were reveling in their visit from Santa and the small gifts each of them had been given.

When a nurse helped Uncle James approach the sleigh to receive his gift, Nick got a little choked up at how frail the old man had become. James hadn't recognized Nick the last couple of times he'd visited, but now he looked Nick right in the eye, his gaze sparkling with recognition.

"You are Saint Nick," he said with a solemn nod.

Nick reached for his uncle's feeble hands. "It's Santa to my friends."

When all of the gifts had been given out, Nick posed for a few pictures, all taken by his helper elf Vivian.

He was relieved when she took his hand and announced that Santa had other places he needed to visit. He smiled and waved and *ho, ho, ho'd* until he was completely clear of the commons room, and then he blew out a big breath that made his snowy-white beard lift right off his chin. His shoulders sagged with relief.

He was thoroughly exhausted, not only physically but mentally and emotionally, as well. Playing one of the world's most recognized characters took a lot out of a guy.

Vivian turned and beamed up at him. "You were absolutely wonderful out there."

"Please don't ever let me agree to do anything like that again," he begged, scratching at a particularly itchy spot on his right shoulder. "I'm more of a behind-the-scenes kind of guy."

"Well, I think it was nice that you did it, especially because I know it wasn't easy for you. It was a true loving sacrifice, and I don't think you'll ever know how many people you touched today."

"Really?"

She nodded fervently. "Really. I know I personally got a little teary-eyed when you read the nativity story."

He scoffed softly, not knowing what to do with the compliment. "Flakes of that fake snow probably got in your eyes."

"I'm serious," she countered. "And what's

more, I think you deserve a reward for all your hard work."

"A reward?" he echoed.

She just smiled and pointed up.

He tilted his head.

Mistletoe.

They were standing directly under a sprig of mistletoe. Had she maneuvered him here on purpose?

Before he could react, she reached up on tiptoe and brushed a soft kiss across his white-bearded cheek.

"Oh," she murmured, clapping a hand over her mouth. "I—I can't believe I did that."

Without another word, she darted off down the hall and then ducked back into the commons area. She knew he couldn't follow her there. Not while he was still dressed in the silly red suit. Clearly she didn't want to be alone with him.

And yet, she'd just kissed him.

He covered his cheek, as if trying to imprint the feel of her lips against his skin. Even if her lips had technically never touched his skin.

Was she sorry she'd kissed him?

He wasn't.

He wanted to kiss her again, a real, lips-on-lips kiss this time.

He mentally poked at the tentative feeling. He'd failed so many times before in his attempts at a relationship. He didn't want to make the same mistakes with Vivian.

He couldn't. It wasn't only his heart he had to consider—or even Vivian's. It was her baby's.

If he were to become invested in Vivian's life—and that was a big *if*—he had to do it right, and he had to mean it. Or not do it at all.

But first he needed to get out of this itchy Santa suit and find the woman.

Chapter Eight

What had she been thinking?

Kissing Nick?

She was an idiot. She'd always been impulsive, giving in to whatever felt right at the moment, but this one took the whole cookie.

That kiss was going to change the entire tenor of their working relationship and the timing couldn't have been worse. With the salon's grand opening less than a week away, she needed to be at a hundred and ten percent, and that wasn't going to happen if she was constantly daydreaming about mistletoe every time she saw Nick's face.

And worse, she had no idea what *he* was thinking. They'd met with the building inspector yesterday and Nick wouldn't even make eye contact with her. After more than an hour of avoiding her gaze and keeping his full attention on the inspector, he'd left without speaking a word to Viv.

Thankfully, the building had checked out. Finally, it seemed like everything careerwise was starting to come together.

Tranquility.

Not that she knew anything about that anymore. She hadn't had a serene moment since the second she'd moved back to Serendipity.

She wondered how Nick would like the name. She hadn't shared it with him yet. She was fairly certain he was still iffy about her beauty salon being successful in a town as small as Serendipity, but at least he'd stopped voicing his qualms out loud.

At the moment, she needed his help more than ever. It was time to let everyone know the date of her grand opening, and that meant posting flyers all over town, talking to other local business owners—especially Jo Spencer, whom Vivian counted on to be a walking, talking commercial for her spa. Viv needed to spread the good news any way she could. She'd just expected Nick to be by her side.

Except Nick hadn't shown up since the

building inspection and she wasn't keen on having to be the one to reach out to him.

She was quite finished humiliating herself, thank you very much. She was afraid to find out what he thought of her now.

She didn't even know what to think of her actions. Maybe it was nothing. Maybe she just had a thing for men in Santa suits.

No. That wasn't it. She could avoid the truth all she wanted and tell herself any number of fibs, but she'd kissed him because he'd opened up his heart and she'd liked what she'd seen.

A man who purposely tried to stay out of the public eye set his personal fears and doubts aside for the elderly residents of the senior center. He'd showed them the dignity and respect they deserved and he had made them feel special. He'd brought them joy and Christmas spirit.

So she'd gotten caught up in the moment and had been carried away by a stray sprig of mistletoe. Who could blame her?

She'd just have to let it go and hope Nick would do the same.

In the meantime, there were flyers to hang up all over town, and if Nick wasn't here to help her then she'd have to do it all by herself.

She started stapling her advertisements to every telephone pole on Main Street. When she got to the end of one side of the town, she crossed the street and moved back toward where she'd started. Afterward she planned to talk to all the neighborhood business owners. Hopefully she'd be able to talk a few into hanging her flyer in their windows or on their community bulletin boards.

Last, she would hit the park, the church and the high school. She had the notion that there were more than a few teenage girls who would want to avail themselves of her services, to get their hair and nails done for a Christmas party or for Serendipity's annual New Year's Eve bash.

Finished with all of the telephone poles, she said hello to the three old men killing time in front of Emerson's Hardware and then ducked into the store.

"Hey, Eddie," she said, greeting the young man behind the counter. "I just wanted you to know that the grand opening of my beauty salon and spa is this weekend." She pressed a flyer into his hand. "I'm calling it Tranquility. Can I count on your support?"

He chuckled. "I've already heard about your grand opening from Nick." He scratched his buzz-cut hair. "I don't think I'll be needing any of the services you offer. Sorry I can't be of more help to you."

Vivian scrunched her brow in confusion. "Nick has already been by here?"

"Yeah. He came by earlier this morning. He made it sound like he was hitting all the businesses in the area. Trying to strong-arm people into coming for opening day, I think." Eddie chuckled.

Nick had already been by? Her heart started warming until the rest of Eddie's words sank in. What was Nick doing? Forcing people to agree to attend her grand opening?

She couldn't even imagine why he thought it was a good idea to compel people to become customers. Surely that would backfire and make folks not want to attend at all.

How could he not know that?

She felt a twinge on her lower back. The baby must be moving about more than normal. She sighed quietly and rubbed the spot with her fingers.

"You're welcome to put up a flyer on our community bulletin board if you'd like."

Vivian offered her thanks, pinned up her advertisement and moved on to the next shop. As she visited business after business, it became apparent that Nick was definitely ahead of her. Everywhere she went, Nick had already been. And it sounded as if he was using the same strong-arm tactics with everyone. At this rate she wouldn't have a single customer who wanted to be there of her own accord.

Maybe that was why the clipboard she'd brought along to sign folks up for services on the day of her grand opening remained empty. Everyone she spoke to seemed to have a reason why they couldn't commit.

Her grand opening was officially going to be a disaster. From the looks of it, she would be standing in an empty beauty parlor on opening day with nothing to do but twiddle her pinkies, while outside people would pass by and gawk at her pathetic little excuse for a spa.

Maybe Nick had been right all along. Maybe Serendipity *didn't* need what she had to offer.

Had she put all of her time, effort and money into her business for nothing?

By the end of the day, she was bone weary and completely discouraged. And as if that wasn't enough, Baby G was evidently trying out for some kind of Olympic tournament. Vivian had been having cramps and spasms all day.

She ended up back at her shop, intending to drop off her empty clipboard and what was left of her flyers and call it a night. Instead, not even bothering to turn on the lights to the building, she slumped into one of her styling chairs, leaned her head back and closed her eyes.

She didn't even hear Nick enter the building until he spoke, causing her to leap halfway out of her chair. She felt like a cartoon cat with its claws stuck in the ceiling and its fur ruffled in fright.

"I see you've got your flyers tacked up all over town." Nick sat in the styling chair next to hers and spun it around with his boots.

She covered her face with her hands. "Don't. Just don't, okay?"

"Don't what?"

"Don't say, 'I told you so.'"

"Okay. I won't. But I'm curious—what did I tell you that I'm not supposed to say I told you about?"

She slid her palms down her cheeks and met Nick's gaze. "Not one. Not one single solitary person signed up to get services on the day of my grand opening. Or any other day, for that matter."

"Hmm." Nick didn't look surprised. Why would he? He'd been calling the salon a failure from day one. Nothing that happened now would be any great shock to him.

"Well, you can sign my mom up for a haircut or something. Jo Spencer, too, I would imagine. And don't forget about Alexis. She's your twin. She has to be there."

Peachy.

While she was grateful for their support, that was three women out of a whole town—one of whom, as Nick had said, would feel she had to be there because she was Vivian's sister. And while Serendipity was small, the fact remained that over half its residents were women—women who were going elsewhere for their salon services.

"Maybe I should just call the whole thing off."

"Why would you do that?"

"Uh—because no one is coming."

No paying customers, at any rate.

"You don't know that."

"Empty clipboard, Nick."

His brow lowered. "This isn't like you. Where's the sunny personality, the-glass-is-always-half-full woman that I'm used to seeing?"

"Right now, I'm feeling partly cloudy with a good chance of showers." She sniffled. She had no intention of crying, not in front of Nick, but despite her best efforts to the contrary, the showers were coming hard and fast.

"Hey." He stood and reached for her hands, drawing her to her feet and into his embrace. He held her tightly, protectively, with one arm around her shoulders and the other spanning her waist—almost as if he were embracing her son, as well.

She breathed deeply of his warm leather and spice scent. She burrowed her head against his chest, reveling in the rumble of his breath and the steady beat of his heart.

She could forget everything when she was in his arms, even her own doubts. She felt safe there. Sheltered. As if nothing bad could touch her, or her baby.

A sound emerged from Nick's throat, somewhere between a growl and a groan. He slid his hand into the hair at the nape of her neck and tilted her head so she had no choice but to look up at him. Even in the meager light, she could see that his gaze had turned dark, the deep blue of the midnight sky.

Vivian couldn't move, or breath, and she couldn't look away from the longing, the silent plea brewing in his eyes.

She should turn away. This—whatever was happening between them now—could be nothing more than chemistry. Hadn't he been the one reminding her over and over of the ways he'd failed in his past relationships? Hadn't he said that he wasn't capable of giving his heart away?

But even so…it had been so long since she'd been held in a man's arms, and she'd never experienced anything quite like the emotions tumbling through her now.

Despite Nick's size, his embrace was extraordinarily gentle, the work-roughened hands he used to frame her face tender. Under her palms, she could feel his shoulder muscles quivering with tension and instinctively knew he was holding himself back, struggling for self-control. He knew her past and was clearly being sensitive to it.

With an unspoken question radiating from his gaze, he gave her more than enough time to react, to pull away, but she could no sooner change what was happening between them than she could stop the world from spinning on its axis.

She would probably regret it. In some ways, she already did. And yet—

She slid her hands from his shoulders down to his biceps and tipped up her chin.

His gaze dropped to her mouth. She trembled as he lowered his head and brushed his lips over hers. His beard was prickly, not anything like the cotton-soft, snowy-white beard he'd been wearing at the senior center, but his lips were gentle as he tentatively explored hers.

She didn't know how she'd come to this point with Nick. They were opposites in every conceivable way. She was an optimist. He was the world's worst pessimist, always considering the bad before the good. She was the owner of a soon-to-open beauty salon and spa. Nick looked like a mountain man.

But as he bent his head and deepened the kiss, none of it seemed to matter. Not their clashes in personality, or their arguments, or even their trust issues.

Tomorrow was soon enough to sort out her emotions. Tonight she needed the comfort Nick was offering her. Being held in his strong arms quickened her pulse. Warmth welled in her chest and spilled out to every corner of her being.

She'd been fighting her feelings for Nick ever since the first day back at the auction. She'd been fighting her fear of being hurt, of heartbreak.

And it wasn't an empty or unreasonable fear—she might get hurt again.

But for tonight, she was going to believe the best about Nick, that his fear of commitment could be overcome, that they could make a relationship work.

Maybe she'd been wrong all along.

Maybe Nick did care.

At first, Nick had taken a dispirited and disheartened Vivian into his arms with no more than the overwhelming need to comfort and protect her, but somewhere along the way, his entire world had shifted.

Maybe it was the sweet, full softness of her lips. Or maybe it was the spring-flower scent of her perfume, or the electricity pulsing across his nerves as her fingers trailed across his biceps. Maybe it was the moment he'd lost himself in the liquid blue warmth of her gaze before he'd kissed her.

But whatever the reason, what had started out as one friend comforting another had quickly sparked into a life of its own, and instead of dousing the flame, he'd stoked it into a raging bonfire that was quickly growing out of control.

It wasn't just the chemistry between them, the way his heart expanded with warmth when Vivian was in his arms.

No—it was so much more than that. He wanted to protect her from the trials she was facing, wipe away her tears, lift her up so she could enjoy the success she'd worked so hard for, the triumph she so richly deserved.

He wanted her to trust him—and he wanted to be worthy of that trust. Was it possible that she could ever trust him with her heart, and maybe even, eventually, with her child?

But how could she, when he couldn't even trust himself? He couldn't ask that of her. It wasn't right—not for her, not for her soon-to-be-born son and not even for himself.

With every day that he spent with Vivian, his heart grew nearer and nearer to hers. The risk of hurting her scared him more than the unlikely possibility of a reward.

The best thing for him to do—the right thing for all concerned—would be for him to step away from this kiss, this project and Vivian's life.

He'd get her through her grand opening and then that was it.

"Vivian," he murmured, his voice thick with emotion as he drew her away from him.

Her cheeks splashed with pink as her eyelids slowly fluttered open.

Oh, but she was beautiful.

Nick wasn't sure he could stand the pain that contracted like a sharp claw around his chest at the thought of not having her in his life anymore.

She smiled up at him. A sound emerged from her throat that sounded like a contented purr.

"I—you—" he stammered, dropping his arms and backing away from her.

Nick threaded his fingers through the thick length of his hair. He could see his reflection in the mirror behind Vivian. He looked like a wild man, and it wasn't just his tousled hair and the dark shadow of his beard.

It was the sheer panic in his eyes.

He swiveled on the heels of his boots, not wanting Vivian to see the truth of his feelings in his telltale gaze. Not now, when she was already under so much stress. Putting anything more on her shoulders couldn't be good for her or for the baby.

He'd allowed his emotions to get the better of him and he was ashamed that he'd led her on, to a place he had no right to go. Somehow, he'd have to make it right, let her down as gently and as painlessly as possible.

She deserved better than what he could offer.

"Nick?"

The hair on the back of his neck stood on end. The way she said his name—

He whirled around to find Vivian clutching the edge of the counter with one hand and her other over her expanded middle. She was half-doubled over and her expression was a mixture of fear and pain.

Instantly, Nick was by her side, one arm around her waist and the other supporting her elbow.

"What's wrong? Is it the baby?"

Vivian nodded and gulped in a sharp breath of air. "I think—"

She cut off her sentence midthought as her brow lowered and she pinched her lips.

Something was wrong. Vivian wasn't due for a few weeks yet. He couldn't remember exactly what she'd said, but he was positive her due date was after the first of the year.

"Should I call 9-1-1?"

She grabbed his wrist. "No. Call Dr. Delia."

"My truck is parked out back. I'll take you straight to the doctor's office and call Delia on the way."

He'd expected her to argue with him as she had the day she'd twisted her ankle in the shop. She'd been so adorably stubborn about it, completely refusing to admit she'd even been in pain, much less that she needed to go see the doctor.

It was frighteningly telling that she merely gritted her teeth and nodded her acquiescence to his suggestion this time. She must really think something was wrong if she wasn't putting up a fight over this.

Continuing to support her at the small of her back and with a hand on her elbow, he gently propelled her toward the back door and then out to his truck, locking the door to the shop behind him.

Three times on the short way out, they had to stop while a wave of pain racked through Vivian's body.

Was this normal? Contractions coming so suddenly, so hard and fast, with very little relief between them?

Nick was no expert by any means of the

word, but he'd always thought that the portrayal of labor and delivery in movies and television shows was unrealistic—sudden, sharp labor followed by a baby born within what appeared to be mere minutes.

He seemed to recall, through the few experiences he'd had around pregnant women, that labor tended to be long and intensive, some lasting for days before the baby was born.

That's not what was happening here. It was more like the movies. Her labor wasn't slow or gradual at all.

Did that mean Vivian's baby was going to be born momentarily? What if he couldn't get her to the doctor's office fast enough?

Panic enveloped him as he opened the passenger side of his truck and scooped Vivian into his arms, gently depositing her into the seat and buckling her seat belt for her.

She didn't speak, not even to protest him hovering over her which, for a chatterbox like Vivian, worried Nick more than anything. She didn't make a sound, other than an occasional soft groan. Not only did she not protest the way he was taking over the situation, but it appeared she was barely aware of what was going on at all. It was as if she'd completely withdrawn into herself. The only thing she seemed to be aware of was the rapidity and strength of her contractions.

Nick slid behind the wheel and revved the engine. His every impulse was to gun the accelerator to equal the race of his pulse, but getting in an accident or being pulled over for speeding by one of Serendipity's finest would only delay their arrival at the doctor's office.

As he drove, he pulled up the doctor's emergency number on the truck's console. Delia's phone rang several times before she answered. With each consecutive unanswered ring, the noose around Nick's heart grew tighter and tighter.

At length she answered, the sound of a dozen people talking and laughing in the background. He felt bad about interrupting a family gathering or party, but his concern for Vivian came first.

"Delia? It's Nick. I'm sorry to bother you at home," Nick said, wondering if his voice sounded as rattled to Delia's ears as it did to his own.

"It's no problem. That's what I'm here for. What's up, Nick?" she asked cheerfully.

"It's Vivian. I'm pretty sure she's in labor right now. I thought maybe I should be taking her to the hospital, but she insisted on seeing you instead. And as fast as this seems to be going, right now I'm not sure she would make it to the hospital before delivering if I tried to get her there."

"Hold on a second." There was a pause while it sounded as if Delia was rummaging around a drawer, probably for a pen and paper.

"How far apart are her contractions right now?"

How far apart? What did that mean? It seemed to him that Vivian wasn't getting any kind of break in contractions at all.

"I'm…not sure? They seem really close together to me."

"Has her water broken?"

Nick nearly slammed on the brakes as his stomach lurched. He was *so* not the right person to be taking care of Vivian in this emergency situation.

Delia chuckled. "It's okay, Nick. Put Viv on the line for me."

"I'm here," Vivian said, her voice low and husky. "Nick's got his truck console on speakerphone."

"Okay, great."

Nick appreciated Delia's calm, collected and reassuring tone. "About how far apart are your contractions, hon?"

"I haven't timed them," she said through a tight jaw. "They are coming pretty quickly, some right on top of each other. Maybe a minute or two apart, otherwise. I'm frightened that there's something wrong with the baby."

"Let's not borrow trouble. I do think, given the circumstances, that it would be best for you to meet me at my office, rather than trying to drive straight to the hospital."

"We're already there," Nick said, cutting the engine in front of the doctor's office.

"Great. I'll be there in five."

Nick turned to assess Vivian. Her head was tipped back against the seat and her eyes were closed. But she looked as far from relaxed as it was possible to get. She groaned and rubbed at a spot on her stomach.

"Should I be reminding you to breathe or something?" Nick had never felt as helpless as he did at that moment, seeing Vivian's pale face in the moonlight, crumpled with anguish. If he could, he would take that pain away from her in an instant and bear it himself. As it was, he was totally and completely useless.

Less than useless. Even thinking about the various elements of childbirth made him queasy and light-headed. He felt itchy all over, as if he were breaking out in hives. His next call was to Alexis, but unfortunately, she and Griff were out of town. He'd have to deal on his own.

He breathed a sigh of relief when he caught sight of Delia's headlights as she parked on the opposite side of the street. He had every confidence that Delia would be able to take things from here and, as an added benefit, she was married to one of the town's paramedics, should it become necessary to transport Vivian and her baby to the hospital.

Please, Lord, don't let it be necessary.

Nick helped Vivian out of the truck and Delia stepped to the other side of her, so they both supported her as they entered the doctor's office. Delia led them straight to the examination room.

"First things first," Delia said in a no-nonsense voice as Nick helped Vivian lay back on the paper-covered medical bed. Delia lightly ran her hands across Vivian's belly and then measured it with a tape. "You're just the right size for thirty-six weeks and four days, so baby is growing just fine. Ideally, we'd like to keep him cooking for another week at least, but if he's ready to make his debut then no worries. Let's get you hooked up to the fetal monitor and find out what this little mister is up to."

Nick cleared his throat. "Should I leave?"

Vivian clenched his hand in hers. "No. Please don't."

Nick pressed his lips into a tight line to avoid showing all the emotions flooding through him. He met Delia's gaze and raised his eyebrows.

Delia smiled in reassurance. Evidently he wasn't as good at hiding his emotions as he'd thought he was.

"It's fine for you to stay right now. In a few minutes I'll have to send you out for a bit, but let's get Vivian comfortable first."

Vivian sighed in relief until another contraction racked through her. Her manicured fingernails dug into Nick's palm but he didn't mind the pain. It gave him something to focus on other than fearing for Vivian and the baby.

"First of all," Delia said, addressing Vivian but with a glance at Nick, "I want to re-assure you that I have delivered dozens of babies right here in Serendipity. And you're far enough along that we should be okay without any special equipment beyond what we've got. So just in case it should become necessary and this little guy doesn't want to wait to be born, we can handle it."

Maybe *Delia* could handle it. But that didn't mean it would be as simple as she was making it sound. Nick could tell she was leaving stuff out—probably a lot of stuff. It unnerved him even further.

"Can you give her something for the pain?"

"We have options," Delia started, but Vivian yanked on Nick's arm and shook her head vigorously.

"No drugs. They would affect my son. I'm doing this naturally."

Nick's gaze flashed to Delia but she merely shrugged.

"We can absolutely handle this exactly the way you'd like, Vivian. Let's figure out how much time we have and then, if we've got enough of a window, we should avail our-selves of my husband's services to get you to the hospital. You've had a completely normal pregnancy, so I don't anticipate any problems with the birth, but at this point the little guy is three and a half weeks early and his lungs might need a little bit of help at first."

The doctor said it so offhandedly it sounded as if it were no real worry, but if it was possible, Vivian's face went a shade paler. Nick's own gut took a hit. Was the doctor saying Viv's baby wouldn't be able to breathe if he was born here in Serendipity tonight?

Delia placed her hand on Vivian's shoulder. "We won't make any decisions until we have a better idea of what's going on tonight, okay, Viv?"

Vivian nodded and then gasped and held her breath as another contraction rocked her.

"Don't forget to breathe through it," Delia reminded her as she attached a fetal monitor to Viv's stomach. "Did you take a prenatal class to teach you how to breathe through your contractions?"

Viv needed to take a class to learn how to *breathe* a certain way? Wow. There really was a lot Nick didn't know about childbirth—and he was absolutely certain he did not want to learn about it just now.

He was forgetting to breathe himself and

was starting to feel a little light-headed, but there was no way he was going to budge from Viv's side. Not as long as she needed him there.

"Is Alexis your birthing coach?" Delia asked.

What was a birthing coach? Nick pictured Alexis with a whistle around her neck shouting plays out of a book but he knew that couldn't be quite right.

"Yes, but she and Griff are out of town for the weekend."

"I see. Is there someone else you could call? I'll be there for the birth, of course, either here or at the hospital, but it's comforting to have someone else by your side to offer you support."

"I could call my mom," Nick suggested. "I'm sure she'd be thrilled to help out."

There was an ulterior motive for Nick's suggestion. If his mom was there, that would give him a good excuse to be there as well—even if it meant driving all the way out to the hospital. If he chauffeured his mom around, he would be there when Vivian's son was born.

And he really wanted to be there when Vivian's son was born.

"That's a good idea," Delia said. "What do you think, Viv? Would you like Nick to call Alice for you?"

Vivian nodded and chuckled through her pain. "I suspect Alice will be able to help Nick, too. He looks a little green around the gills."

Nick made a face at her but by that time she was deep in the midst of another contraction and had once again retreated inside herself.

"I'll just step out and call my mom," he said.

"Good. That will give me the opportunity to examine Vivian. I'll let you know when you can return to the room."

Nick breathed a sigh of relief when the door closed behind him and he was alone in the waiting room. He removed his hat and scrubbed a hand through his hair.

How had everything gone so wrong so quickly? It was only days before the official grand opening of Tranquility—the name he'd seen on the flyers she'd made—and weeks before Baby G was supposed to be born. And now suddenly Vivian had started labor.

Had he somehow caused her premature labor?

He'd seen the stress and discouragement in her gaze when he'd met her back at the salon earlier that evening. She'd been convinced her grand opening was going to be a complete and utter failure. Which was an unfortunate and unexpected byproduct of a plan he'd worked up.

If only she knew. The complete opposite was true. The whole town was coming out for Vivian's big day. He'd worked hard to make sure it happened. He'd hoped to give her a nice surprise with his efforts.

Instead, Vivian was lying in the room next to him strapped to a fetal monitor and very likely soon to give birth to her premature son.

He fished his cell phone out of his pocket and speed-dialed his mother, who answered on the first ring.

"What's wrong, Nick?" she asked in lieu of "hello."

He hadn't expected that, and her question completely threw him off his game. "What makes you think something is wrong?"

"Because you never call me unless you need something." She couched the accusation in a loving laugh. "So what is it this time?

You don't know how to boil artichokes? You just turned your white T-shirts pink?"

"It's Vivian," he said, tossing his hat onto an end table and slumping into the nearest chair. "I'm pretty sure she's in labor right now. And I think it's all my fault."

Chapter Nine

❧

To Vivian's relief, her contractions had slowed and become irregular, not to mention far less painful.

"Everything looks fine," Delia assured her. "False alarm this time. They are called Braxton Hicks contractions. Your body is practicing for the main event. Your baby will probably be born right on schedule."

"*Practice* contractions? I am going to hate to see what the real contractions feel like."

On one side of her, Nick squeezed her hand. On the other, Alice patted her shoulder reassuringly.

"We women have toughed it out and delivered babies since the beginning of time," Alice reminded her. "I know it seems impossible to imagine right now, but no matter how bad the labor pains are, once they put your sweet little baby boy in your arms, you'll know he was worth every last contraction."

"But that won't be for a few weeks yet," Delia assured her with a smile.

"And the funniest thing of all is that the good Lord gives us selective memories," Alice continued. "Even the memory of the pain will be mostly forgotten. And it's a good thing, too, or Nick would have been an only child."

Vivian glanced at Nick, expecting him to laugh and come back with a quip about the hassle of being raised with Jax and Slade, but to her surprise, he was frowning, his brow lowered over stormy blue eyes.

"Could these—what did you call them? 'Fake contractions?' Could they have been brought on by stress?"

Delia's gaze widened. "Possibly, but it's highly unlikely. Braxton Hicks are just a woman's body preparing for the real thing. And as Vivian here can tell you, sometimes they can feel quite real and be every bit as painful as a true contraction, but they're not really a sign that anything is wrong. Sometimes it's nothing. Sometimes the baby is slightly out of position and the mom's body is making some last-minute adjustments."

"I imagine she has been under a lot of stress," Alice murmured. "What with the grand opening of her beauty salon right around the corner. Have you been working yourself too hard, sweetheart?"

Vivian opened her mouth to speak but Nick beat her to the punch bowl.

"Yes, she has. She spent all day today on her feet, plastering advertisements all over town. I doubt she even took time to sit down and eat lunch."

Vivian bristled. Of course she'd eaten. She'd gotten a corn dog to go from Jo's Café, along with a bag of sour cream and onion potato chips. Her eating habits didn't even remotely resemble her prepregnancy fare, but then, little did, these days.

"Vivian, I'd like you to stay another half hour or so just to make sure we're clear of all contractions. And then I want you to take it easy. I know you've got your grand opening coming up, but try to rest if you can and stay off your feet as much as possible."

Delia removed the straps of the fetal monitor, but when Vivian tried to sit up, Delia laid a restraining hand on her shoulder.

"Keep resting for me for a little while longer, will you, hon?"

Vivian took a deep breath and then sighed. She would rather have gone home to her own house and not have everyone fretting over her, but she supposed it was good that they cared.

Alice had even offered to attend the actual birth, being an extra support person along with Alexis. Vivian had gratefully accepted. It felt nice to have a mother figure by her side, especially since her own mother had passed away from cancer when Viv and Alexis were only six years old.

"I guess I'll be on my way, then," Alice said, kissing Vivian's cheek. "But you make sure to have Nick program my cell phone number on your speed dial. Feel free to call me day or night, and it doesn't have to be because you are in labor. I'm always happy to talk."

"Thank you. Really, Alice, I can't tell you how much your support means to me."

Alice patted her arm. "I know, dear. I know. As of this moment you can consider the whole McKenna clan as family, can't she, Nick?"

Nick made a choking sound. Even through

the scruff on his cheeks she could see the heat rising to his face. Alice's words had probably embarrassed him, poor man. Even so, they were welcome to Vivian's ears.

Nick cleared his throat. "I'll walk you out to your car, Mama. And, Delia—if I could speak to you for a moment?" He nodded his head toward the waiting room.

Vivian laid with her hands clasped around her middle, staring at the ceiling. Her silly baby had apparently gone to sleep, now that the excitement was over.

It felt like quite a bit of time had passed, and Delia and Nick still hadn't returned. What was taking them so long? Were they still in the waiting room? Would they mind if she came out there, too? Viv hadn't had a single contraction in over an hour, and she badly needed to use the facilities, which were located off of the waiting room.

Finally, half out of curiosity as to where Delia and Nick had disappeared to, and half because the baby was now awake and was currently using her bladder as a trampoline, Viv rolled off the narrow bed and opened the door to the waiting room.

To her surprise, Alice hadn't left yet. She

appeared to be deep in a hushed conversation with Nick and Delia.

Vivian didn't know whether it was the tone of their voices or maybe their postures, but something made her freeze in the doorway without making her presence known.

"So then, you want me to be there a little before ten o'clock?" Alice asked, clearly confirming something Nick had said earlier.

Nick nodded. "I told Vivian I'd signed you up for a haircut so she'll be expecting you. The official opening time is at ten, so any time around there should be fine."

Vivian cringed. They were talking about her—and her hopeless grand opening. Of course it would be fine if Alice arrived just as the door opened. It wasn't as if there was going to be a huge line waiting for Viv's services.

"And what about me?" Delia asked. "Did you want me there a little before ten, as well?"

Nick shook his head. "No, you don't have to come—"

Vivian gasped and clapped a hand over her mouth. She ducked back into the examination room, all thoughts of leaving for home or using the facilities instantly evaporating.

She suddenly felt as if all the air had left the room. She was shaking so hard her teeth were chattering.

Nick was actually telling people *not* to come to her opening instead of urging them to come? Why would he do that?

She slipped back onto the exam bed and turned toward the back wall, curling into a ball. If only she could disappear from here and not have to face Nick—or anyone in Serendipity—ever again. She was just so, so tired and disheartened.

"Vivian?" Nick's deep voice came from behind her. A moment later she felt his large, warm hand on her shoulder.

Why did he have to be so gentle? Tears pricked Vivian's eyes.

"Are you all right?" he asked, having the gall to sound genuinely concerned.

Vivian knew she was trembling under his touch but she couldn't seem to help herself. She'd never been so angry in her life—not even when she'd discovered the cattle lounging inside her shop.

She'd been angry with Nick then, too, and had immediately blamed him for the whole incident. And then she'd had to ask for forgiveness because he hadn't been at fault.

But this time there could be no doubt. It would be hard for her to misinterpret Nick's words to Delia.

No. You don't need to come.

"I thought I might have heard you a minute ago but I must have been mistaken," Nick said.

Vivian didn't trust her voice to answer.

"Delia says you can go home whenever you'd like, but I'm not in a rush if you still want to rest for a while. Take all the time you need."

He sounded so sweet. So gentle.

So sincere.

How could he act this way when her world was about to break into tiny, irreparable pieces? Is that why he'd asked about stress bringing on labor? Because he already knew how the grand opening would turn out?

Little did he know—and neither had she, until this moment—that the worst part wasn't that her business had been set up for failure.

It was that Nick had concurred.

She'd *trusted* him. With her business, her friendship and even, perhaps, eventually with her heart. She'd been starting to feel like her emotions were healing, that she might be able to fall in love again and that this time that love might last forever.

She'd thought Nick was different. Certainly her feelings for him were unlike any she had experienced before.

How could she have been so wrong?

DUMB AGAIN !

Nick really had his work cut out for him. Vivian had managed to staple advertisements to every single telephone pole in Serendipity, and that was to say nothing of all the community bulletin boards and shop windows. She was nothing if not thorough.

There couldn't possibly be a single resident in Serendipity who didn't know about Tranquility's grand opening, and that meant trouble for Nick.

Folks around here would welcome any excuse for a party, and they especially liked it when they were able to help their neighbors at the same time. That's why the Bachelors and Baskets auction had been such a success, and the opening of the senior center, as well.

Now, with Tranquility's grand opening…

How was he supposed to put that kind of fire out? It was the day before the grand opening and he'd heard the buzz about town. He could only hope Vivian hadn't.

He'd tried to stay a step ahead of her and make sure everyone was hush-hush about his surprise for the event, but even one person letting the cat out of the bag would be one person too many, and enough to ruin all his plans.

He tried to open the back door to the salon, but it was locked. He was surprised Viv wasn't here yet—putting all of the finishing touches on the place, giving the floor one last mop, shining the mirrors until they sparkled, arranging the stock of premium products that had only arrived yesterday.

For the past week, Viv had been busy training her two new protégés, Nicole and Lauren. She'd barely spoken a word to Nick. In fact, if he didn't know any better, he might have thought she was purposely avoiding him.

He put his key into the lock and flipped on the lights as he entered the building. It looked perfect—just as perfect as his plan would be...he hoped. There had been a moment that night in Delia's office when he'd been certain his plan had been uncovered. In hindsight, it hadn't been such a great idea, discussing his strategies for the grand opening with his mom and Delia when Vivian was potentially within hearing range.

He'd been concentrating so hard on the mechanics of getting the right people to show up at the right times that it hadn't even occurred to him that Vivian might walk into the waiting room and ruin the surprise altogether.

At one point he'd heard what he thought was a gasp and his heart had leaped into his throat, but when he'd whirled around, expecting to see Vivian, he'd found the examination room door closed. And when he'd returned to the exam room, Viv was still lying on the bed, so all was well.

He was grateful he'd just imagined it. Talk about a way to take all the fun out of the secret.

Still, Vivian was acting odd around him—and when she finally arrived, it only got worse. He told himself that she had too much on her mind—preparing for the grand opening and for Baby G's imminent arrival.

She barely spoke to him, and when she did, it was to order him about, telling him to do this or that. Gone was the sweet, sensitive Viv with a ready smile and a tinkling fairy laugh. In her place was a frowning woman with drooping shoulders and black circles under her eyes.

It was clear she wasn't following Delia's suggestion to rest more and put her feet up.

"Are you getting enough sleep at night?" he asked her, cornering her as she stocked new product onto the front shelves. She shrugged rather than answered.

He grabbed an armful of red shampoo bottles with long, pointed nozzles and started placing and facing them next to the shelf where Vivian was working.

He tried again. "Are you overexerting yourself? The doctor said you shouldn't be pushing too hard. You need to think about the baby."

"I'm fine," Vivian snapped, scowling at him. "And I *am* thinking about the baby. Why do you think I'm working so hard to get my business up and running?" She pulled the bottom corner of her full lower lip between her teeth. "Don't nag me. Who made you the sleep police?"

"I'm just concerned. You know what Dr. Delia said."

His initial reaction was to snap back at her. But that was just one of the many ways he had learned and grown through his relationship with Vivian. He now tried to give more thought to his words and his attitude before he spoke. He tried to consider the other person's feelings first, and tried to discern what God would want him to say or do. Right now Vivian was clearly testy because she was stressed about the grand opening. She still deserved gentle treatment and compassion, even if she wasn't in the right state of mind to show those qualities herself.

And hadn't Vivian been the one to teach him the old adage that you could catch more flies with honey than with vinegar?

Although knowing Vivian the phrase would come out something like catching more hummingbirds with honey or flies with jelly in that delightful way she had of mixing her metaphors.

In any case, the good old Golden Rule applied. Do to others whatever you would have them do to you.

And if he felt half as physically and emotionally wiped out as Vivian looked he wouldn't want someone pushing his buttons, intentionally or not.

Vivian made a hissing sound through her teeth. "Yes, yes, I know. I'm sorry. I didn't mean to harp at you. It's just that I can't finish all the last-minute details of the grand opening if I'm lying on my couch with my feet propped up."

"Okay." He wanted to tell her she could always ask for his help...but he knew it wouldn't do any good to argue with her when her will—and her jaw—was set. "But at least tell me what I can do to make things easier on you."

Vivian had been facing a row of premium conditioners, but suddenly her hand jerked away and four bottles fell clattering off the shelves.

He immediately reached down to retrieve the bottles, knowing how difficult it was for her to pick things off the floor in her current expanded condition.

As soon as he straightened up, she wrenched the conditioners from his grasp. "I think you've already done enough."

He felt as if there was an entirely different conversation going on between them, in a silent language that he had no idea how to translate.

What did she mean? They'd been working together on this project since day one, when she'd bid on him at the auction. And now all of the sudden he'd *done enough*?

What was that supposed to mean? He certainly didn't have a clue. And it was difficult not to get his back up when she continued to talk in riddles.

"We'll be good to go if we work together on this." He was frustrated beyond belief but he focused all his energy on keeping his tone mild.

She just stared at him as if he'd suddenly sprouted a pair of horns.

Or maybe that look meant she wanted him to disappear.

Well, he could do that, he supposed, and make one more pass around the neighborhood, reminding everyone when they should arrive for the grand opening.

"Okay," he concluded.

"Okay?" He thought he saw a flash of distress cross her gaze before irritation replaced it.

She wanted him to leave, but she didn't really want him to go? He wasn't about to try to solve that particular female quandary.

"Okay, I'll leave, if that's what you want," he clarified. "But not until we've taped the butcher paper over the front windows. That's a two-person job and I don't want you climbing any ladders."

She opened her mouth to protest and then

promptly closed it again. He was right and they both knew it, so there was no use in her arguing with him.

The butcher paper had been his idea, and one of his brighter ones, he thought. It was ostensibly to hide the interior of the finished salon from prying eyes until it was revealed during the official grand opening, but really it was a way for him to mask what would be happening on the street outside the shop.

"I don't know why we're bothering," Viv said as Nick used packing tape to secure the butcher paper to the top of the window. "Anyone who wanted to could already have looked in the window for the past few weeks and seen all the new fixtures." She shook her head. "Not that anyone would want to see the inside of a beauty salon."

He wanted to argue with her, or shake some sense into that stubborn blond head of hers. Didn't she realize what an amazing job she'd done? She'd made the beauty parlor as beautiful as she was.

This pessimism was so not the Vivian he knew and...*liked*. It was as if someone had switched off the light inside her.

This whole idea of his wasn't working out the way he had planned it at *all*. Or rather, it *was* working, but he hadn't planned it very well or considered all the contingencies he might encounter.

She just had to last until tomorrow.

So did he. Because right now, seeing her downcast face, he was an inch away from blurting out the whole truth himself.

But at this point he might as well keep his mouth shut and let things unfurl as they would. She was kicking him out of the salon early, anyway. The next time he saw her, he would be able to make everything in her world right again. Her downcast features would turn to delight and happiness.

Whether or not she ever forgave him for his subterfuge and the unnecessary pain he'd caused her was another thing entirely. After everything was out in the open, she still might never want to speak to him again.

And even if everything went off without a hitch, even if Vivian was as shocked and delighted as he hoped she would be, and even if the sequence of events erased the strain between them, their relationship would still never be the same again.

Because after tomorrow, he'd have no real reason to seek Vivian out anymore. He'd be of no use to her. More than that, he wasn't good enough for her and her baby. Sure, they might remain friends on some level and exchange pleasantries at church or social events, but it wouldn't be the same. He wouldn't be seeing her every day and working together with her, and that thought gripped painfully at his chest.

Her sunshine had finally started to seep into his cold heart. What would happen to him when the clouds returned?

No doubt about it. There were dark days ahead. But he would take comfort in the fact that Vivian, at least, would be basking in the balmy glow of happiness and success, with her thriving business and her healthy baby boy.

Seeing Vivian happy, even from a distance, would have to be enough for him. She and her son deserved the very best that life could offer them, and, as he'd once again proven by this botched-up grand opening scheme, he was not it.

And he never would be.

Chapter Ten

Vivian took extra care in her appearance, gussying up in her most fashionable dress and styling her hair for the special opening-day event. She didn't know why, considering she was entirely convinced no one would attend her grand opening—well, except those who had been coerced into being there. Her sister, Jo Spencer and Alice, since Nick had signed her up to get her hair done.

Even if she was dressing only for the few people who would take the time out to visit her, she wanted to look her very best. She had very little pride left, but if she was going to fail, she would go out looking her best.

As she curled her hair into soft waves, she thought about what she was going to do next. All of her plans since the moment she'd returned to Serendipity had revolved around remodeling the beauty salon and planning for her grand opening.

But if the salon failed, then what was next for her and her son?

She hated to have to think about letting Nicole and Lauren go so soon after hiring them. What a disappointment that would be. But if she didn't have the work for them, she wouldn't have money to pay them, and for their sakes, it would be better for them to pursue their careers elsewhere. They deserved more than the measly tips they would receive in a town too small to really warrant a salon and spa.

She was convinced now more than ever that Nick had been right all along.

She met her own gaze in the mirror. "That's enough of that negative thinking," she admonished her reflection. "Chin up, smile on your face. Even if it's just a few loyal friends, they still deserve your best efforts."

She'd been through what she'd thought were impossible circumstances before, when she'd discovered she was pregnant and Derrick had abandoned her. She'd survived, and she would walk through fire to the other side this time, as well.

In any event, she had the birth of her precious baby to look forward to. She couldn't wait to meet her son and hold him in her arms.

And it wasn't as if she would starve. She was one of the blessed ones, and she thanked God for it. She had family, and they wouldn't let her down. Alexis and Griff would support her for as long as she needed to get back on her presently pregnancy-swollen feet.

And rise, she would—although she would be doing two months of Alexis's laundry in addition to her own. Her soon-to-be new arrival would create even more laundry for her.

The thought made her chuckle.

"See?" she told the mirror. "There's humor to be found in any situation if you look hard enough, no matter how grim it might appear on the outside."

Her chuckle turned into full-blown laughter. She wasn't usually in the habit of speaking out loud to herself in the mirror.

She pulled her hair back and tied it up with a soft lavender-colored ribbon.

There, then. She'd done her best. There was no use putting off the inevitable.

She drove down Main Street on her way to the salon. Serendipity wasn't a busy town in general, but today it was even quieter than usual. Quite vacant, actually, especially for a Saturday. Even the three old men in the bib overalls who were usually a firm fixture on their rocking chairs in front of Emerson's Hardware were noticeably absent.

It figured. She wouldn't even be able to use her status as a local oddity to draw in foot traffic today.

She pulled her car around to the back alley where the shopkeepers tended to park. Nick's truck was already behind the salon but there was no sign of him.

Not surprisingly, the back door was unlocked. Nick was sitting in one of the styling chairs. His head was back, his eyes closed, and his hands were clasped across his muscular chest. His black cowboy hat was tipped low over his brow and his breath was coming slow and even, as if he was napping.

He looked completely relaxed. If he wasn't asleep then he was close to it.

It figured. Well, she was glad *someone* wasn't stressed out about the way this day was going to play out.

"Didn't get enough sleep last night?" she remarked wryly.

He tipped his hat back with his fingers and grinned broadly, his blue eyes clear and sparkling.

"On the contrary," he said. "I slept like a baby, and then I was up with the dawn, well rested and raring to go. I was feeling antsy, so I decided to come on by the shop early. I rearranged the stock room and labeled all the shelves so it will be easier for you to find specific products when you need them. Alphabetical order. That seemed to be the most logical way to go."

"You did *what*?"

He held up his hands as if to stave off the dressing down he'd clearly realized she was just about to give him.

"Before you start squawking, at least take a look at it. If you don't like how I've stocked everything I'll rearrange things however you want."

"The stock room is the least of my concerns," she said, looking around the salon. She tossed a glance over her shoulder. "And I don't squawk."

"We did good, didn't we?" He came up behind her, near enough to touch her. She could feel his breath fanning her cheek, but he kept his arms at his sides.

It *was* good. She was proud of how the remodel had turned out, with its relaxing lavender-painted walls and glistening gray-tiled floor. Soft instrumental music piped through the room, adding to the feeling of—

Tranquility.

"Where did all the flowers come from?" she asked, just now noticing the vibrant bouquets of fresh flowers in vases at every styling station.

"Oh, that's nothing. I thought the scent of fresh flowers would make the salon distinctly—I mean, well—" He stammered to a halt and lifted his hat, threading his fingers through his thick hair.

"Distinctly—?" she probed.

"Your, uh, perfume reminds me of spring flowers," he blurted out. "I wanted Tranquility to smell like you."

Her eyes widened and warmth bloomed in her heart. That had to have been the sweetest thing anyone had ever done for her, bar none. She didn't even know what to say.

"That was…very thoughtful of you."

He'd gone to all the trouble of buying fresh flowers because they reminded him of her?

It was nearly an hour's drive to a floral shop, which was the only place a man could get so many bouquets at once.

She would almost have thought he was rooting for the grand opening to be a success, if she hadn't heard words from his own mouth to the contrary.

Nothing made any sense right now.

Nick glanced at his watch. "Only half an hour to go. Are you getting excited?"

"I'm not sure it's hitting me yet," she said honestly. "It doesn't feel real."

She was counting the minutes, but not the way Nick was probably imagining.

Nicole and Lauren arrived, bubbling over with excitement and chattering up a storm. It was bad enough that Viv was anticipating her own crash and burn without bringing the girls into it. That was the real shame.

"Oh, to have the energy of youth," she murmured, stretching and rubbing the small of her back. "I feel like I'm over the mountain."

Nick burst into hearty laughter. "You're hardly over the *hill*, Viv."

"Well, I feel like it right now."

Nick's gaze narrowed on her, assessing her. "You're still carrying too much weight on your shoulders. I told you that you should rest more."

She crinkled her nose at him. Resting more was simply not in her vocabulary. Not now.

"Did anyone ever tell you that you're stubborn?" Nick asked rhetorically.

She shrugged. "It might have been mentioned once or twice over the years."

"Well, I, for one, admire that trait in a woman."

What? That wasn't what she'd expected him to say. She'd thought he was gearing up to insult her.

He made a sweeping motion with his arm. "It takes real guts and determination to take an old, run-down shop and turn it into this. It's incredible."

"Yeah, Viv, it looks amazing," Nicole said.

"Beautiful," Lauren agreed.

Nicole was scheduled to work the mani/pedis while Lauren was doing facials. Today, Vivian was supposed to be the one doing haircuts and perms on the clientele.

Supposed to be being the key words.

"It doesn't matter how nice it looks without guests around to enjoy it."

"Then I guess it's time to let your new customers see what all this fuss is about." Nick walked to the front window and grasped the edges of the butcher paper.

"Are you ready?" he asked, glancing backward and flashing Vivian a toothy grin.

Despite knowing there was probably hardly anyone outside and no reason to hope for better, Viv inhaled deeply and held the air in her lungs. A sense of giddy anticipation filled her chest.

"Drumroll please." He ripped off the paper in one smooth motion. "And... Tranquility is officially open for business. Vivian, will you do the honor of flipping the sign on the door from Closed to Open?"

She let out her breath in an audible *whoosh*.

Instead of the three or four people she had expected, Main Street was packed, lining both sides of the street for as far as Viv could see. Some of the ladies from the altar guild at church had set up a table and were selling baked goods. It looked like a party.

Her party.

"What?" she breathed, her heart welling at this unexpected outpouring of love, kindness and support from her friends and neighbors. It looked as if the whole town had turned out for the grand opening.

Nick chuckled. "I doubt if you're going to

be able to cram all these guests into one day. I'd hazard a guess and say you've probably got a good month of work ahead of you, and that doesn't count repeat customers, of which I'm sure you'll have plenty. I wouldn't be surprised if you are thoroughly booked when you get back from your maternity leave."

Vivian could hardly believe what she was seeing, but Nick was right. Tears of happiness and gratitude poured down her cheeks.

"I can hardly believe my eyes!" With a squeal of delight, she launched herself into Nick's arms and hugged him tightly. He laughed and swung her around.

She could have kissed the man. In fact, she might just.

"Surprised, darlin'?"

Surprised didn't even begin to cover it. Alexis, Jo and Alice each had a clipboard and were making their way through the crowds of the people she'd spoken to as she'd canvassed all the neighborhoods. She even spotted Eddie Emerson, joking around with a group of his friends.

Never in her wildest dreams could she have imagined that so many people would turn out to support her, to make Tranquility a success.

The expression on Nick's face was one of sheer pleasure and appreciation. He was relishing the moment as much as she was. When their gazes met, she could see pride there, too. But she was confused. Hadn't Nick been against her plans? She'd heard him tell Delia not to come to the grand opening. Delia apparently hadn't listened to him, because she and her husband, Zach, were hanging out at the front of the line, chatting with some friends.

Nothing made sense anymore.

"I suppose we'd better get busy," Nick said.

"We?" It sounded as if he was taking mutual ownership in Tranquility. She supposed in many ways the small shop was as much his as it was hers. The majority of the remodeling had been done by his hands. But she couldn't even fathom the change that had come over him. Did he really want the salon to be a success, after all?

"That's right," Nick affirmed. "I'm going to be running the cash register today—oh, and manning the phone. I imagine it will be ringing off the hook before long. That way you three lovely ladies can focus on beautifying Serendipity."

Vivian was certain she was gaping, especially when Nick flashed her another one of his heart-stopping grins.

In one smooth move, he tossed his hat on the hat rack in the front corner and opened the door. The first folks in line were clamoring to get in. Jo and Alice barked out orders like a couple of kindergarten teachers rounding up children after recess.

Vivian expected Nick to step away from the door once he had opened it. He'd said he was going to man the cash register and the phone.

Instead, he was blocking the entrance completely, his large, muscular frame filling the doorway.

Leaning a shoulder against the door frame, he raised his brows as if he was waiting for something.

"Nick?" she asked, once again confused by his actions.

"Where do you want me?"

Was this a trick question?

"Behind the cash register?"

"Well, sure, I'm going to man the register for you for most of the day. But not yet. I'm going to be the first one in line to get—" His throat clogged and he had to stop and clear it. "I'm going…" he said again, in a steadier voice "…to get a haircut."

Vivian gasped. The girls giggled. Nick lowered his brow and marched determinedly to the nearest styling chair and sat down with a little more force than was strictly necessary, sending the chair spinning.

Could it be that she was not going to have to do two months of Alexis's laundry, after all? She wanted to crow in exaltation.

His fingers were clenched to the arms of the styling chair and his jaw was taut with strain. If Vivian didn't already know better, she would have thought the man was getting ready for a dental procedure, staring up at a novocaine syringe and a whirring drill.

Maybe a little nitrous oxide would help take the edge off the poor man's agony, for he was clearly in excruciating pain.

The very thought of having to use laughing gas to get Nick through a haircut sent her into a spasm of giggles. She covered her face to mask her amusement.

"That's a sight we won't see too often," Jo said, entering the salon and tossing her fully filled-out clipboard onto the front desk next to the register. She was wearing one of the homemade T-shirts she was known for. This one proclaimed It's a GRAND Day!

"I'll say," Vivian agreed.

"Maybe we should take a picture of him and frame it so we can hang it on the wall at the café."

That nearly sent Vivian into another fit of laughter. She was seriously struggling to regain her composure, but she couldn't help an occasional little snort from escaping her lips.

Nick cleared his throat—loudly.

"If you ladies are finished having fun at my expense, I would appreciate getting this over with. I would like my hair cut now, please. I'm sure the people waiting in line behind me are anxious to have their turn to be tortured."

Vivian wrapped a cape around Nick and laid her hands on his shoulders. "Would you like me to give you a shampoo and conditioning treatment? It's free with a haircut today."

She literally felt him cringe.

"Okay, then," she said, knowing better than to push for too much. Reaching for the spray bottle, she misted his hair with water. "What would you like done today? A little off the top?"

It took him a moment to answer. "I have

no idea. Whatever. Just please don't cut my ears off."

"I think I can promise that won't happen," she said with a laugh. "Do you want a shave, as well?"

He frowned and tilted his chin from side to side, examining his reflection. "I guess."

She picked up her comb and shears and met his gaze in the mirror. "You know this doesn't hurt, right?"

He huffed and crossed his arms underneath the cape. "Speak for yourself."

She combed through Nick's thick hair and pulled the first section between her fingers. Her shears were posed for the first snip, but something stopped her.

Here she was, one clip away from having two months of laundry done for her—so why was she hesitating?

Nick seemed willing—if grudgingly so. But even though he was making no move to get away, she knew he'd probably rather be pretty much anywhere else in the world right now. Yet he was here, making the sacrifice.

The town gossip mill would definitely be ruminating over this day for a long time to come—which Vivian knew was the whole point. The transformation of Nick McKenna was nothing to take lightly.

And when everyone saw the way her styling techniques made a new man of him, a man who could step off the pages of a fashion magazine, the line outside her door would never cease.

Her business would be an overwhelming success.

One snip and she'd be on her way.

Nick desperately tried to look as if none of this bothered him, but given the fact that all of the women in the room were laughing at him, he figured he'd pretty much failed at his attempt to remain cool and collected.

This was silly. It was just hair. And it wasn't as if he *never* visited the barbershop— just maybe not as often as other guys did.

What he didn't like was getting all froufroued up with most of the town watching like he was some kind of sideshow act. Who knew how many people were gawking at him from outside the store window?

Which was the whole point, but that felt irrelevant at the moment. He was *trying* to make a spectacle of himself, get everyone's attention so he could prove Vivian's talent was worth her weight in gold.

What better way than to let her turn him from a beast into—*ugh*. What *was* she going to turn him into? He didn't even want to think about it.

Maybe it would be less painful if he just closed his eyes.

Vivian ran her fingers through his hair. He couldn't hear the snip of scissors, and yet he imagined lengths of it were floating down to cover the shining gray-tiled floor.

Viv was unusually quiet, though. Whenever he visited the barbershop, he'd always found it almost obnoxiously loud, full of men shouting and laughing and jibbing each other.

He supposed he'd thought a beauty salon would be even noisier, given that women liked to gab so much.

But it was strangely silent in the room. Was it supposed to be this way? Maybe the spa would live up to its name, after all.

Curious, he opened his eyes. Vivian's gaze wasn't on his hair. She was staring at his reflection in the mirror, her comb and shears still poised for action.

Suddenly, she dropped her arms and slid

the instruments of torture into the pockets of her apron.

He lowered his brow. "What?"

She merely smiled. "You're done."

"What?" He looked in the mirror, confounded. What was the woman talking about? He couldn't see any difference at all. And when he glanced at the floor, it gleamed back up at him, free from all traces of hair.

"You haven't done anything yet."

"Exactly."

"But I thought—"

"You have no idea how difficult this is for me." She groaned. "Just so you know, I'll be washing Alexis's laundry for two solid months because of this."

"Now you've really lost me."

Viv sighed dramatically. "I *may* have mentioned to Alexis that I could get you cleaned up by the end of the day of the grand opening and that if I did, she would do my laundry for two months."

"Cleaned up," he repeated. His gaze widened. "And then if you didn't, you have to do two months of *Alexis's* laundry."

"Something like that."

He pressed his lips together to keep from

laughing, but in the end he had no choice but to give in to it.

"You certainly like a challenge, don't you?"

"It makes life interesting."

Challenges certainly *did* make things interesting, and Nick had never known a challenge quite like Vivian Grainger.

"So let me get this straight. Alexis will have to do your laundry if you manage to make me look like a dull lawyer instead of a rowdy rancher?"

"Well, I hope it wouldn't be as bad as all that." She stepped back and folded her arms over her rounded belly.

"If that's what you need to do then I don't mind," he said.

He felt like he was a specimen under a biologist's microscope.

"No, I don't think so," she said at last. "You're good to go."

Nick spun his chair around. "Come on, Vivian. You have the opportunity here to get back at me for all the grief I've caused you—not to mention getting free laundry service for two months. How can you pass up on that?"

He'd been thinking of Slade and the calves when he'd spoken and thought she would be laughing at the reference, but instead, a moment of anguish flickered in her eyes. She masked it quickly, but not fast enough. He knew her too well.

"What's wrong?"

She looked as if she was about to say something—something serious—but then she apparently thought better of it. She smiled and gestured to the waiting line.

"If we're through here, you're holding up my business."

He stared at her for a moment, completely baffled, but then he nodded. "Right. I belong behind the cash register."

The rest of the day went by in a whirl of familiar faces, names, cash transactions and credit card swipes. Nick was new to the appointment software but it didn't take him long to pick it up. And thanks to Jo, Alexis and his mom, he and Vivian would have to work after-hours entering all the appointments folks had signed up for on the clipboards. The calendar went out for at least two months, and that was without repeat customers.

Nick couldn't have been more pleased with the overwhelming success of Tranquility's grand opening. Vivian beamed with delight when lines of people filed through to congratulate her on her new business and wish her well.

The altar guild made a killing on baked goods. A win-win, as far as Nick was concerned. They kept the ravenous hoard filled with sweets while the church's donation box was filled with stacks of dollar bills.

The grand opening celebration was supposed to go from ten in the morning until five o'clock at night, but it was well after six before they were finally able to turn the door sign from Open to Closed.

Vivian immediately dismissed Nicole and Lauren, thanking them for all their hard work and sharing with them excitement at the future of Tranquility.

As if there had ever been any question about it.

Nick couldn't believe he'd ever given Vivian such a hard time about her plan, especially in the beginning. Of course Serendipity needed a beauty salon. Everyone needed their hair cut now and again, and why shouldn't the ladies of Serendipity pamper themselves with a manicure or a facial?

Vivian had been right and he had been

wrong, and he was man enough to admit it. More than that—he was happy to admit it.

"Unbelievable," Vivian said, slumping happily but tiredly into one of the styling chairs. "I honestly thought my grand opening was going to be a complete disaster."

"I was afraid you might be worried about that, although scaring you wasn't intentional on my part. I didn't realize when I started all this that my actions would cause equal and opposite reactions."

"Chemistry?"

"Physics." He shrugged. "I excelled in the sciences in high school, but when it comes to real life, my little experiment started bubbling over and I didn't know how to keep it from exploding."

"I heard you talking to Delia and your mom about the grand opening the night we were at the doctor's office."

"I thought I heard you come into the waiting room that night, but when I turned around, the examination room door was closed, and when I looked in on you, you were resting quietly. I decided I must have been mistaken."

"I didn't want you to know I'd heard what you said. You really hurt my feelings."

"No, wait. If you heard me talking to my mom and Delia, then you would have known about the big surprise I had planned for your grand opening."

Her brow lowered and he thought she might have winced. "That's not what I heard."

He was trying to follow the gist of the conversation, but somewhere along the way he'd become completely lost. He backtracked to the last place he had seen tracks, where he had any idea what they were talking about.

"Vivian, what exactly do you think you heard me say that night?"

"I believe your exact words to Delia were, 'You don't need to come.' I don't think that's open to more than one interpretation."

He chuckled. So that was what this was about. He'd started to think he'd dug himself in so deep that he'd never get out, but *this* he could handle.

"It might have changed your interpretation if you had stayed around long enough to hear the entire sentence."

"What does that mean?"

She shifted in her chair, looking as if she was unable to find a comfortable way to sit. Nick imagined it probably would be difficult for her to get comfortable while carrying around an almost full-grown baby inside her. She was getting bigger every day, but not in a bad way.

"What it means is that you didn't hear what I really said to Delia, which was that she didn't need to come *at the same time as my mom did.* I was afraid if too many people came early to the event, they'd start making too much noise and you'd figure out what was happening. I didn't want you to know how big of a crowd awaited you until I pulled the butcher paper down from the windows. That was supposed to be the surprise."

Tears filled her eyes.

"So the reason you were canvassing the neighborhood ahead of me was in order to plan this…surprise party."

"Guilty as charged, although I never meant for you to get hurt in the process."

"Unbelievable."

"I know. I'm sorry."

"No, it's not that. I'm the one who should be apologizing to you. Once again, I automatically jumped to the wrong conclusion about you, and I should have known better. I'm so ashamed of myself for being so distrusting. You deserved better from me. You have repeatedly shown me that I can depend on you, and what do I go and do? Leap to all the wrong conclusions. Again."

She reached for his hand. "I should have trusted you, Nick, and I'm sorry I didn't."

His chest warmed, expanding until he thought it might burst, and his heart leaped into his throat.

She trusted him?

"Thank you," he said, his voice gravelly. "You'll never know how much those words mean to me."

She smiled softly. "Oh, I think I do."

They were silent for a moment, each lost in their own thoughts. Vivian shifted in her chair several times before attempting to stand.

Even that movement was complicated. She braced both hands on the arms of the chair and strained to achieve the forward momentum she would need to roll out of the chair, but to no avail.

He stood and reached out his hands to her, giving her the leverage she needed to rise.

She groaned and then made a deep, eerie moaning sound that echoed throughout the salon.

"I feel like a beached whale," she explained when he looked at her funny.

"That was supposed to be a beached whale?" He chuckled. "You sounded more like a mummy."

"I suppose that's apropos," she said, joining in his laughter. "Since I'm going to be one of those soon, too."

He rolled his eyes.

She paced slowly back and forth across the room, stopping from time to time to stretch and rub the small of her back. Nick suspected she'd overdone it today, and she had definitely been on her feet too much.

"We have an impressive list of new clientele to enter into the appointment database," Nick told her. "I don't know about you, but I'm too exhausted to tackle that project tonight."

She fought back a yawn and nodded. The dark circles under her eyes told Nick more than any words she could say.

"It's nothing that can't wait," he assured her. "But if today was anything to go by, I think you may have to consider hiring an assistant to make appointments, man the cash register and answer the phone."

She leaned against a counter and smiled weakly. "It's incredible, isn't it? The outpouring of love and support the community gave me?"

"I'm not surprised."

"I can't believe I need to consider hiring another employee. When I woke up this morning I thought I was going to have to let Nicole and Lauren go."

"Well, you can put all those worries to rest. Your biggest problem now is counting your piles of cash. And then put some of that money toward bringing in an assistant to take some of the work off your shoulders. Now that the grand opening is over, I expect you to follow Dr. Delia's orders and put your feet up more often."

"Bossy much?"

"My brothers probably thought so when we were growing up together."

Their gazes met and held. Nick felt as if all the oxygen had left the room. She was so beautiful.

"But this isn't me trying to be dictatorial," he continued. "It's me worrying about you and Baby G."

She broke eye contact with him, staring out through the front glass into the darkness beyond.

"I'll be all right. It's not your job to worry about me, Nick."

A lance pierced his heart. What did she

think? That after all of these months working together, he could just set his feelings aside and walk away from her? Didn't she realize how much he cared for her?

"I really appreciate all the help you've given me," she continued, "both in remodeling my salon and everything you did to make my grand opening a success."

She still wasn't looking at him, and her words sounded very much like a brush-off.

It was happening again.

"I was glad to do it."

What else could he say? His emotions were in turmoil.

"It'll be kind of weird not having you around here, but I know you must be anxious to return your full attention to your ranch."

That was the truth. He'd been neglecting his ranch in favor of helping Vivian.

Now he was going to have all the time in the world to ride the range and care for his cattle.

And think.

Alone.

That one word held a lot of impact.

Not so long ago he was comfortable being by himself, didn't see the need to seek out others for company. And then he'd been bought at auction by a vivacious woman who'd showed him that there was so much joy to be had in opening himself up to the world. It wasn't going to be so easy this time to hibernate on his ranch and keep his head stuck in the sand.

"I guess we'll still see each other at church." His voice broke on the last word.

Her gaze returned to his. Large droplets of tears illuminated her impossibly blue eyes, making them into infinitely deep wells. He could happily lose himself in that gaze for the rest of his life.

Was she feeling the shock of their future separation as much as he was?

Was there another way?

"Vivian," he began, not sure how to ask the question that was burning inside him. He desperately needed an answer, but was almost afraid to hear what she might say.

He reached for her, but she stiffened in his arms. Had he been reading the signals all wrong? Seen what he wanted to see in her gaze, heard the longing he was feeling in her voice rather than truly noticing what she was trying to convey?

"Viv, I—" he started again.

Vivian trembled and grasped at the material on the front of his shirt.

"I've been trying to ignore this all day," she said in a ragged whisper. "I thought maybe if I didn't acknowledge it, it would go away."

A chill skittered up Nick's spine. Was she speaking of her feelings for him? Had she, like he had, come to the place where she could no longer deny her emotions?

He framed her face with his palms, allowing his joy to run free, wanting her to see the love in his eyes.

But her gaze didn't mirror his.

Her expression was tight with pain and her eyes full of agony.

"Nick," she said on a groan. "I think I'm in labor." She puffed out a breath. "For real this time."

Chapter Eleven

As excited as Vivian was to meet her son and hold him in her arms at last, getting to that point ended up being a lot more time-consuming and complex than she'd anticipated.

All through the day of the grand opening, she had been experiencing twinges and minor cramps, but they were nothing compared to the Braxton Hicks episode she'd had earlier, and so, in the excitement of the day, she'd ignored them.

But what had started out feeling like a dull backache had progressed through the day until, by the time the last guest had exited and she'd changed the sign on the door to Closed, the contractions had become quite regular and she could no longer ignore them.

They started at about fourteen minutes apart and then gradually grew closer together.

Nick had immediately panicked when she'd informed him that she was in real labor, insisting that she sit down and rest while he made the necessary phone calls.

Even as distraught as he appeared, Vivian was glad to have Nick with her. He was a take-charge kind of man, and for all that she teased him about it, his ability to put plans into motion was very handy.

He'd called Dr. Delia first and had Vivian talk through all her symptoms and everything she was feeling. These contractions were different. Deeper and more regular. Delia assured her that first labors were usually quite long, but because Serendipity was so far from the nearest hospital, Delia told Nick to take Vivian there immediately, promising that she would meet them there.

Nick called Alexis and Alice and told them the news, and then tenderly supported Vivian as they made their way out to his truck. His attention and hovering was adorable. She couldn't bring herself to let him know that she was perfectly capable of walking on her own, and that in the space between her contractions, she really wasn't in a lot of pain.

So instead, she let him fuss over her and enjoyed the extra attention. He drove to Alice's house first and they exchanged Nick's truck for Alice's more comfortable sedan.

As they drove to pick up Alexis, Alice took the wheel, while Nick sat in the backseat with Vivian, holding her hand and talking her through her contractions. In between, he cradled her in his arms and whispered encouragement to her.

At his mother's urging, Nick used the stopwatch feature on his cell phone to time the length of her contractions and how far apart they were.

At first, Vivian had picked up on the anticipation and adrenaline of the moment, but it wasn't long before the pain started to wear on her. She was already bone weary from a long day and she couldn't seem to find any position that was comfortable to sit in for any length of time.

And then there was her underlying fear—she wasn't yet thirty-eight weeks along, which was technically the earliest date to be considered a full-term birth.

By the time they got to the hospital, Vivian barely knew what was happening, other than what was going on within her own body.

Nick tried to pull into the emergency parking lot, but Alexis assured him that Vivian would be better cared for if they used the hospital's main entrance and went directly up to the maternity ward.

Nick found a wheelchair just inside the main door and gently settled Vivian into it, wrapping her in his warm sheepskin jean jacket. The jacket smelled like him, all leather and spice, and the familiar scent helped to calm her.

From there it was all a blur. Triage, being hooked up to a fetal monitor when she really wanted to move around. She missed Nick's presence when he was herded off to the waiting room, but Alice and Alexis were right by her side, holding her hands and reassuring her that all was well.

After several hours of labor, in which Baby G wasn't making the progress Delia would have liked—Vivian, too, for that matter—Viv was convinced to get an epidural. She'd simply been too tired to continue the fight without assistance.

After the epidural had been administered

and Vivian was able to relax, her labor sped up again, and before long she heard the blessed sound of her son's first cry.

Georgie, as it turned out, wanted to greet the world sunny-side up, which Delia said was probably the cause of her severe Braxton Hicks contractions as well as why her labor had taken so long.

Nick visited the moment he was able. His eyes were glowing with amazement when Vivian passed little Georgie to him. The baby looked so tiny in Nick's huge hands, and yet Vivian knew there was no safer place her son could be.

"Hey, there, Georgie," Nick crooned in the high voice men used with babies.

He grinned at Vivian. "He looks just like you. Blond hair. Clear blue eyes. Cute little wrinkled nose."

Vivian smiled, her heart full to overflowing.

"Is Georgie a family name?"

She shook her head and laughed. "No. But I'd been calling him Baby G for so long that it only seemed right that I gave him a name that started with the letter *G*."

"I like it."

Vivian didn't know why Nick's opinion mattered so much, but it did.

"He came out full-sized and healthy, but the little brat was sunny-side up," Vivian told him.

"What does that mean?"

"Most babies are born facedown. The first anyone saw of Georgie was his smiling face."

"That's proof positive that he's your son." Nick gently placed the baby back into Viv's arms.

"Yes, but it made my labor longer and more complicated."

"Is it true what my mom said? That you forget all about the pain after the baby is born?"

She snorted. "Well, I don't know about that, but I do know that having Georgie was worth any amount of pain."

"When are they cutting you loose from this joint?"

"Tomorrow morning."

"Good. My mom will be here to take you home, okay? I've got some things to do and Alexis says she needs to get a head start on your laundry."

"But I didn't win the dare."

"She saw me cave. She said that was good enough for her."

Vivian chuckled. She didn't want to admit that she'd hoped Nick would be the one bringing her home. After everything that had happened, she just wanted to be with him.

Back at the salon there had been a moment when she'd thought she glimpsed the same emotions she felt in his eyes, but she must have been mistaken if he was so quick to leave her and Georgie's sides.

She tucked her heartache aside as she spent the rest of the day learning how to care for a newborn baby. She'd been worried that she might not be a natural mother and was surprised and relieved at how easily changing and feeding Georgie was for her.

As promised, Alice arrived first thing the next morning to await Vivian's release from the hospital. Alice had become more and more of a mother figure to Vivian and she didn't know what she was going to do when she was no longer involved with the McKennas. They really had become like family to her.

Alice slowed her sedan as she entered the long driveway of Alexis and Griff's ranch property. Vivian was currently staying in a small cabin on the outskirts of the ranch, at least until she could make other arrangements—which, happily, she would soon be able to do, since the salon was taking off so well.

"Are you ready to introduce baby Georgie to his new home?" Alice asked, her voice lined with excitement.

"Oh, yes. And to show him off around town."

Alice turned the curve just past Alexis's main ranch house and Vivian caught the first glimpse of her own little cottage.

She gasped in shock. Multicolored helium balloons were bobbing everywhere, along with an enormous blue banner with baby footprints and the words Welcome Home, Vivian and Georgie.

Tears filled Vivian's eyes as she saw all the people waiting on the lawn for her. Not only were Alexis and Griff there, but all three of the McKenna brothers, their significant others and their children.

Nick stood on the walk in front of the cabin, an enormous bouquet of red roses in his hand.

As soon as Alice pulled to a stop, Nick strode forward and opened the car door, gesturing to the scene before her.

"Welcome home, fair princess and little prince. Your family awaits."

Nick's eyes were alight with joy as he handed Vivian the flowers and unbuckled the baby from his car seat.

Family?

Yes, this very much felt to Viv like a family scene, and for the first time, she released all the fear and tension she had that she alone would not be enough for her son.

She didn't need to be worried, for Georgie would be surrounded with love and care.

"Thank you all," she whispered, her voice cracking. "This is so far beyond anything I could ever have imagined."

"That's not all," Nick said, taking her shoulder and turning her toward where Slade and Jax stood shoulder to shoulder.

When they backed away from each other, Vivian saw what they had been hiding behind them.

The little red tricycle, all repaired and cleaned and gleaming in the sunlight. The spokes had been straightened and the streamers on the handlebars had been replaced, as had the little bell. It had a fresh coat of red paint and the chrome had been polished.

Vivian exclaimed in delight. "Oh, Nick. How did you know?"

He chuckled. "You didn't think I noticed that you kept taking the trike out of the junk pile? After a while I got the hint."

She put her free arm around his waist and hugged him tight.

He cleared his throat. "You might want to look a little closer."

Intrigued, she turned her gaze back to the tricycle and realized it wasn't just the silver spokes, polished chrome and bright red paint that was catching the sunlight.

There, on the seat, was an open black velvet box. Inside was a beautiful diamond solitaire.

She clapped a hand over her mouth and her tears fell freely.

Nick reached for the box and knelt before her.

"I wanted our families to be here to share in our joy," he said, smiling up at her. "Little Georgie will always have plenty of family to dote on him."

Vivian knew Nick was making her a promise.

She nodded, trying to breathe, trying to

swallow, but her head was spinning and nothing seemed to be working.

"Vivian Grainger," Nick said, holding Georgie in one arm and extending the ring in his other. "I love you. And I think I've loved Georgie even before we formally met. Will you do me the very great honor of becoming my wife?"

She couldn't see through her tears and she couldn't speak, but she nodded and put out her left hand.

When Nick slid the ring on her finger, it was as if every fear, every concern, vanished like mist in the morning sun.

He stood and embraced her. "I want you to know that you and Georgie will always be safe, protected and cared for, as long as I'm around. You've both stolen my heart."

"Oh, Nick." She reached her hand up and brushed her palm over the sweet, scratchy beard that was Nick McKenna. "I love you, too. I have for a long time, I think. You've already given me so much. I can only hope I can make you happy for the rest of our lives together."

"You already have," he said huskily, and brought his lips down on hers.

Their families hooted and applauded but

Vivian was too wrapped up in Nick—and their future together—to really notice.

When she hadn't even been looking, love had crept up on her, and finally her heart was experiencing what she'd been searching for all along.

Tranquility.

Epilogue

Christmas Eve had always been one of Nick's favorite times of the year. He always enjoyed the children's nativity pageant and the midnight candlelight service at the church.

This year, however, topped anything he could ever have imagined. He couldn't believe all the blessings he'd received.

He had thought he was meant to be alone. Now he had a beautiful fiancée and her bouncing baby boy to make his life complete.

And tonight was special in another way. Nick's heart beat in anticipation as he sat with his family in the darkened church with nothing more than the glow of candles for light.

The choir started the hymn, slowly and reverently.

Silent night. Holy night.

Nick joined in, his baritone mixing with the other voices. He smiled at his mother. Her heart was healing. Although she still grieved for her departed husband, she had started living her life again.

There was a soft gasp and Nick turned to the back of the sanctuary, where Vivian was slowly walking up the aisle. Soon, she would be walking up this very same aisle to tie her life to his, but tonight she had another important role to play.

She was dressed in a blue robe with a white mantle, and in her arms she carried a swaddled, sleeping Georgie.

When she reached the front of the church, she laid Georgie in the life-size manger and knelt next to him, softly joining in with the others to sing the rest of the hymn.

Nick was so proud he wanted to burst. His heart swelled so much he thought he might not be able to endure the sweet tenderness.

Georgie's very first Christmas pageant, and he had landed the prime role.

Baby Jesus.

* * * * *